SISTER I

'I need a career of my own!' Jane Marshall tells brilliant young Dr Mark Frobisher. But he doesn't agree, and so ends their romance.

Eight years later, *Sister* Jane Marshall finds that she's to work with the same Mark Frobisher on his Hong Kong project. And this time there's certainly no room for romance between a liberated career girl and an old-fashioned doctor!

*Books you will enjoy
in our Doctor Nurse series*

SISTER IN HONG KONG

BY

MARGARET BARKER

MILLS & BOON LIMITED
15–16 BROOK'S MEWS
LONDON W1A 1DR

*First published in Great Britain 1984
by Mills & Boon Limited*

© Margaret Barker 1984

*Australian copyright 1984
Philippine copyright 1984*

ISBN 0 263 74842 1

Set in 11½ on 12½ pt Linotron Times
03–0984–41,000

*Photoset by Rowland Phototypesetting Ltd
Bury St Edmunds, Suffolk
Made and printed in Great Britain by
Richard Clay (The Chaucer Press) Ltd
Bungay, Suffolk*

CHAPTER ONE

THE PLANE seemed as if it was about to plunge into the sea. Jane held tightly on to the sides of her seat and closed her eyes. In spite of the successful career girl image she always portrayed, she had never got over her fear of flying. It was a necessary part of her life now, but she still felt as if she was that young student nurse who had gone on her first flight over to Jersey for a week's holiday with her mother.

'You need a break, darling,' her mother had said. 'All that work on the wards, and the exams. We'll have a lovely little holiday away from it all. You've been looking very tired lately; you'll feel much better when you get back.'

But Jane hadn't felt better after the holiday. In fact she had felt worse, because by the time she got back to St Catherine's hospital the man she loved had flown off to America and she knew she would never see him again. It was all such a long time ago . . .

The plane shuddered a little. Jane allowed herself to open one eye, and then two. The beauty of that blue, blue sea fascinated her so much that, momentarily, she forgot her fear.

The plane was skimming along only a few feet above the water, preparing to land on the narrow airstrip that projected out into the Bay of Hong Kong. Jane held her breath; there was a slight bumpy feeling as the plane touched down and then it was taxiing along the runway.

She looked out at the bright sunshine glinting on the roof of the airport and couldn't help remembering that eight years ago she might have flown in with Mark beside her for their honeymoon. As a newly-qualified doctor of twenty-four, he had seemed so mature to her in those days—and so devastatingly handsome. It had been love at first sight for both of them, and their whirlwind romance had swept Jane off her feet. After only three weeks Mark Frobisher had asked her to marry him and fly out to Hong Kong for their honeymoon. Mark's parents were living out there, and he had wanted to show her how beautiful it was. Jane remembered that fateful weekend when she had dashed home excitedly to see her widowed mother.

'But Jane—you're only eighteen,' her mother had said. 'You've got all your life in front of you! Don't tie yourself down to the first man you meet. I've had such a struggle to bring you up on my own. A woman needs qualifications nowadays—you've got to be a person in your own right . . .'

Well, she *was* a person in her own right now,

and had been for some time. She remembered going back to hospital, seeing Mark, and asking him if they could wait until she had finished her training—only three years.

'Only three years?' he had echoed. 'That's a lifetime! I need you with me now. I'm going to the States soon—it's the chance of a lifetime, I've got my career to think of . . .'

'Yes, and I've got mine' she had retorted. 'I'm a person too; I need a life of my own. Can't you see that?'

'Yes, I can see that now,' he had replied, quietly. 'Don't worry, I won't interfere with your life any more.'

'But Mark, I love you,' she had faltered lamely.

'Do you?' Those marvellous blue eyes had pierced inside her. 'You don't know the meaning of the word love. You're too young. Perhaps we're both too young,' he had said, almost to himself.

The next month had been agony for Jane. Whenever she saw Mark it was in a professional capacity, or else in the company of the vivacious Dr Cynthia Martin, who had trained at St Catherine's with Mark. They had both left for the States while Jane was on holiday with her mother. Shortly after Jane returned, the news filtered through the hospital grapevine that Cynthia and Mark were engaged. Jane felt as if a knife had been twisted inside her, but it was a turning point in her life.

That's it, she had told herself; now I've *got* to have a career. She had worked steadily and single-mindedly in everything she had taken on. And her mother was so proud of her. It was because of her efficiency and dedication that she had been asked to take on this important Hong Kong assignment. But every once in a while the same dull, familiar ache would come back into her life, like now, as she went through the plane doors and out into the exotic and exciting atmosphere of Hong Kong, remembering what might have been.

In a way I'm going to exorcise the remains of that long-ago romance, she thought, as she firmly adjusted her shoulder-bag and walked with a purposeful stride to the baggage-reclaim area. That little part of my life that keeps cropping up, like a feeling of nausea in the pit of my stomach, is going to be banished forever.

The suitcases came slowly along the rotating baggage strip; they were all shapes and sizes. Jane's suitcase was expensive, like everything else she now owned—the outward sign of the successful career girl. It's good to be independent, she thought. If I'd come out here with Mark I would have had to take second place to his career. Then, without warning, a second thought came into her mind. We were going to spend our honeymoon at his parents' beautiful beach house at Sheko, where the waves pound against the rocks . . .

Don't be so childish, she told herself. You're a grown woman and there's no time for daydreams in your life. Her leather suitcase was coming slowly along the baggage strip. She reached forward, picked it up and headed for customs.

She was soon through and on to passport control. The young immigration officer looked at her appraisingly as she handed him her passport. He studied her face much longer than was necessary, noting the dark, well-cut hair, the high cheek-bones, and the vivacious green eyes. Then his eyes travelled slowly over the tall, slim, elegant figure in the cream linen suit, before glancing briefly at her passport.

'Are you here on business or pleasure, Miss Marshall?' he asked with a bright smile.

'I shall be working here for six months,' said Jane, aware that the people in the queue behind her were beginning to get impatient.

'I see,' he said in a leisurely fashion, unwilling to miss the chance of exerting his full authority with such an attractive young lady.

'And what is the nature of your work?' he asked, trying to assume a professional voice.

The man in the queue behind Jane breathed an audible sigh of weariness and banged his suitcase down on to the floor. Jane took a deep breath and patiently began her explanation, conscious now that all eyes and ears were upon her.

'Well, as you can see from my passport, I'm a nursing sister. I've been asked to take charge of the nursing aspect of Cheung Lau project.'

'The Cheung Lau project?' asked the immigration officer.

'It's a clinic which has just been started on Cheung Lau island,' replied Jane.

'And who is financing this project?' he persisted, still smiling.

'I'm afraid I have no idea,' replied Jane, as patiently as possible. 'At the hospital I was merely informed that some rich, philanthropic businessman was financing a much-needed clinic on one of the islands near Hong Kong. My only concern in the project is of a medical nature.'

'Of course.' The officer closed Jane's passport and reluctantly handed it back to her. 'I hope you will enjoy your stay in Hong Kong,' he added courteously.

'Thank you, I'm sure I will.' Jane gave a brief smile of relief that the interview was over and picked up her suitcase.

Outside, the sun was unbearably hot as she walked to the edge of the pavement. A bright red taxi pulled alongside almost immediately and the driver leapt out so that he could put her suitcase in the boot. Thankfully, Jane sank into the back of the car.

'St Margaret's hospital,' she said to the driver, who quickly let in the clutch and roared off through the traffic at breakneck speed. They tore through the crowded streets, and Jane was amazed at the way a pathway cleared miraculously as they surged forward. She had a blurred vision of cars, bicycles and crowds of people in brightly-coloured clothes, all thronging the roadside. On either side she could see exotic and colourful shop windows, displaying every conceivable kind of marketable goods. Before long the taxi slowed down to go through the tunnel which takes the traffic from Kowloon under the water and out to Hong Kong Island.

When they emerged on the other side the car started to climb up through the busy streets. Jane was fascinated to see old-fashioned double-decker trams bumping along down the middle of the road, alongside the very latest and expensive saloons.

As the taxi climbed higher up the hillside road towards the peak, Jane could see more and more of the harbour, in which floated vessels of every kind. There were junks, sampans, sailing-boats, fishing-boats and enormous yachts. The Star ferry was halfway across the bay, ploughing its way from the mainland of Kowloon to Hong Kong Island. The road to the peak seemed never-ending as it wound its way higher and higher on and then all at once it flattened out into a wider stretch leading to the hospital. They drove through the wide gates and up to the main entrance. Jane suddenly felt slightly nervous, but she put a stop to that by asking the driver how much she owed him in her phrase-book Cantonese.

'*Ng Goi Mai Dan*,' she said very slowly. He smiled at her and replied in perfect English.

Oh well, she thought, perhaps I'll be able to get by over the language problem more easily than I anticipated! She handed over the necessary Hong Kong dollars.

'Thank you very much, madam,' said the driver politely. He carried her heavy case into the main entrance, then with a brief smile he hurried back to his taxi.

'Can I help you?' the receptionist at the main desk asked brusquely.

'Yes please, er,' Jane looked around nervously and then remembered to put on her mature, professional voice. 'My name is Jane Marshall; I believe Matron is expecting me.'

'Yes, of course, Sister.' The receptionist's attitude changed completely. 'Would you care to take a seat? I'll tell Matron you're here.'

Jane sat down thankfully as the receptionist picked up the phone. 'Sister Marshall is here, Matron,' she announced, and then after a short pause she turned to Jane. 'Matron will be with you in a moment, Sister.'

Jane looked around her at the huge windows which looked out over the Bay of Hong Kong, and thought what a superb position it was for a hospital. A plump, mature lady with twinkling eyes and wearing a navy blue dress and white starched cap came briskly into the hospital foyer and Jane stood up to shake her outstretched hand.

'Sister Marshall, how very nice to meet you. I'm Matron O'Sullivan. I trust you had a good journey.'

'Yes, thank you, Matron,' Jane replied, noting the attractive lilt of Matron's Irish accent.

'Good, good! Well, I'm sure you'd like to have a look round our beautiful hospital. Miss Smith will take care of your luggage.' She beckoned to the receptionist. 'Have one of the porters take Sister Marshall's luggage over to the nurses' home.' Then she turned back to Jane. 'Did you know you are to spend the first two nights here at St Margaret's, Sister?'

'No, I didn't—I thought I was going to . . .'

'Not to worry,' Matron interrupted. 'It's all arranged. You'll need a couple of days to recover from your flight. You may feel all right now, but jet lag has a way of creeping up on you when you least expect it. You must have an early night, of course.'

'Of course,' Jane found herself saying. She suddenly began to feel tired, but was sure it had nothing to do with jet lag. It was a long time since she had met an old matron like this one. Probably the salt of the earth, but terribly wearying. It reminded her of her days in the preliminary training school at St Catherine's.

'Now come along, Sister, follow me,' Matron was saying as she set off at a quick pace down the corridor and out on to a balcony where five female patients were sitting in easy chairs, enjoying the late afternoon sun.

'This view is quite breath-taking, Matron,' said Jane.

'Yes, isn't it?' Matron smiled her approval at the remark. Then, turning to the patients, she asked, 'How are we today, ladies?'

Various replies came from the patients simultaneously, so that it was impossible to decipher what each one had said. Matron, however, was not simply being polite. She went from patient to patient, making a de-tailed check to ensure that everyone was com-fortable. And it was obvious that the patients adored her. When she was quite satisfied that all was well, the guided tour continued through several small wards and private rooms until they reached the operating-theatre. This was obviously Matron's pride and joy and she had been saving it until the last.

'This was completely rebuilt last year,' she said proudly. 'We can now handle any oper-ation. I can't take you into the theatre at the moment, but I'll show you into the ante-rooms.'

She pushed opened the swing-doors and led the way into the shiny new operating wing. A couple of nurses in white uniforms burst into a frenzy of activity as Matron appeared.

'Nurses, this is Sister Marshall. She's come out from the UK to look after the Cheung Lau project,' Matron announced.

'How do you do, Sister,' said the nurses politely, and continued to busy themselves preparing trays of instruments for sterilising.

'There's an emergency appendicectomy going on in there, otherwise I could have taken you round,' Matron continued. 'Perhaps tomorrow, if the list is finished in the morning . . .' She broke off in mid-sentence as the doors to the theatre opened and the tall figure of the surgeon emerged. He was peeling off his gloves and the two nurses rushed to help him. His eyes above the white mask looked across at Matron and her visitor.

Jane's heart missed a beat as she saw those piercing blue eyes. It couldn't be! No it couldn't be . . . The surgeon pulled off his mask and Jane gasped. Fortunately Matron had started to prattle on again and nobody noticed Jane's confusion.

'Dr Frobisher, this is Sister Marshall, newly arrived from the UK. She's going to supervise the nursing staff at the Cheung Lau clinic.'

Matron turned to look at Jane. 'Dr Frobisher is in charge of the project.'

'How, er . . . How interesting,' Jane smiled briefly, hardly daring to look at Mark.

'It was fortunate that you were here just now Dr Frobisher, so that I could make the introductions.'

'Hardly introductions, Matron,' replied the surgeon. 'Sister Marshall and I have already met. We were both at St Catherine's.'

'Well, what a coincidence! That will make working together so much easier for you,' Matron said.

The nurses had untied the strings at the back of the operating-gown and were waiting for Matron to go so that they could remove it.

'Well now, I think we'd better leave you,' said Matron, sensing that her presence was holding up the proceedings. 'Perhaps you'll take tea with us later, Dr Frobisher,' she added.

'I doubt it, Matron,' he said quietly without taking his eyes from Jane's face. 'I'm going to have a shower and then I've got a lot of work to do.' Abruptly he dropped his professional manner and smiled. It was the old, familiar, dazzling smile that made Jane feel weak at the knees. 'You've changed,' he said to her.

'So have you,' she replied in a shaky voice, aware that Matron was now watching the pair of them intently.

'You're more—sophisticated,' he said with a sly, boyish grin.

'Eight years is a long time,' Jane replied quietly. 'You wouldn't expect me to stay the same.'

'No, I wouldn't,' he admitted coldly.

There was a brief moment in which it would have been possible to hear a pin drop. Time seemed to stand still—then Mark suddenly turned and walked away from them.

'If you change your mind about tea, Doctor . . .' Matron started to say, but he cut her short.

'Sorry, Matron, some other time. I'm too busy now. Goodbye, ladies,' he said as he went through into the shower area.

Jane felt unexpectedly dizzy. The room seemed to be spinning round. She put out a hand to hold on to something and Matron was by her side at once.

'My dear, you've gone quite white! Must be the jet lag. I told you it would catch up with you. Nurse, bring a chair quickly! There my dear; sit down here, that's better.'

Matron continued to fuss as Jane closed her eyes and tried to make sense of her confused thoughts. Whatever was Mark doing here in Hong Kong? She had always thought he was still in the States!

'What you need is a strong cup of tea, my dear. Then we'll take you over to your room for a nice rest.' Matron's voice, seeming so far away, penetrated her thoughts. 'Are you feeling stronger? Ready to stand up? Good, good. Come along then, Sister. Lean on me if you feel faint again. Fourteen hours in a plane, not to mention the change of time and the unaccustomed heat—well, it's enough to make anybody . . .'

Jane allowed the comforting monologue to waft gently over her as she obediently walked beside Matron down the corridor towards the staff common-room. She felt like a young student nurse again, helpless, vulnerable and desperately in love with a newly-qualified young doctor.

Matron opened the door of the common-room and the spell was broken. Jane forced herself to return to the present, to her career girl image, her professional manner. As she walked through the door, several pairs of eyes were immediately upon her, taking in the well-cut suit of Matron's tall, attractive guest. Jane followed Matron across the large, airy room to a group of sisters sitting out on the balcony.

'Ladies, this is Sister Marshall who's just arrived from the UK. Suffering a little from jet lag, I'm afraid, but we all know about that, don't we? Sister Marshall, this is Sister Benson, Sister Jones and Sister Ko.' The sisters started to move the chairs to make room for Matron and Jane around the table and

Sister Benson went off to fetch some fresh tea.

'Did someone tell me you are here to help with the Cheung Lau project?' asked Sister Ko, smiling amicably at Jane.

'Yes, I've been seconded here from St Catherine's in London for six months,' Jane said.

'St Catherine's?' murmured Sister Jones enquiringly. 'Isn't that where Dr Frobisher trained?'

'Yes, it is,' said Matron. 'Now isn't that a coincidence?' She turned to Jane, asking quite innocently, 'Did you know each other well?'

'Oh, Dr Frobisher was already qualified when I started my training so we only coincided for a matter of weeks, as I remember.' Jane said confidently, now fully in control of the situation and completely at ease. 'What a splendid view you have up here on the peak. It must be very healthy for the patients.'

'For the nurses, too,' laughed Sister Benson as she set the teapot down on the table. 'I just couldn't go anywhere else in the world after this place, and I've travelled quite a bit.'

'Do I detect an Australian accent?' Jane smiled.

'You do indeed,' replied Sister Benson proudly, as she poured out the tea. 'The finest country in the world! But we haven't got a view like this, so I'm going to stay put, even though I do miss the kangaroos.'

They all laughed and Sister Benson handed round the teacups.

'We're a very international hospital,' said Matron. 'Sister Jones is from Wales, Sister Ko was born here in Hong Kong, and of course you would never be able to guess where I come from,' she added, deliberately exaggerating her accent.

'Never in a million years, Matron O'Sullivan,' smiled Sister Benson. 'One day you must give us a little clue.'

They all laughed again, and Jane found herself warming to the friendly atmosphere of the place. She took a sip of tea and began to feel much stronger. They had been chatting for several minutes when the door opened and a woman in a white coat stood in the doorway, looking around the room as if she was trying to find someone.

'Dr Martin,' called Matron, 'come over here. I want you to meet Sister Marshall.'

Jane turned as the pretty, fair-haired doctor crossed the room. Matron was already performing the introductions.

'Dr Cynthia Martin, this is Sister Marshall.'

'How do you do?' Dr Martin smiled and shook hands with Jane. As she did so Jane noticed the broad gold wedding-ring on her finger.

'Don't I know you from somewhere?' asked Dr Martin, looking slightly puzzled. 'Have we met before?'

'Quite possibly,' Jane said. 'I trained at St Catherine's, but I was only a young student nurse when you went off to America.'

'Yes, now I remember! I never forget a face, although you've changed considerably—you're more sophisticated.'

'That's exactly what Dr Frobisher said,' laughed Matron.

'Oh, he *would* say that,' Dr Martin said with a laugh.

'Cup of tea, Cynthia?' asked Sister Benson.

'No thanks, Helen. I must dash. I only dropped in to see if Mark was here.'

'No, he's only just come out of surgery,' Matron said helpfully. 'You might catch him down in theatre.'

'Thanks, I'll nip along there now . . .' and Cynthia hurried away.

'I must go back to my office,' Matron announced. 'Would one of you ladies take Sister Marshall to her room in the nurses' home? She looks all-in.'

'Certainly, Matron.' Sister Benson jumped to her feet. 'I'm off duty for a couple of hours.'

'Well, I'll say goodbye for now,' Matron said to Jane in a kindly voice. 'Do get some rest and have an early night. I'll see you tomorrow.'

'Yes, of course Matron,' Jane smiled. There was an almost audible sigh of relief as the older woman swept out of the room.

'Phew, what a woman!' muttered Sister Benson. 'She's got a heart of gold, but she does go on a bit, doesn't she? Shall we go, Sister Marshall?'

'Call me Jane, please.'

'I'm Helen,' said Sister Benson. 'And this is Wendy Jones and Grace Ko. We can dispense with the formalities now that Matron's out of the way. She really is a dear, but she's twenty years behind the times. Knows her medicine though—you can't catch her out on any of the new techniques. I guess she spends all her spare time with her head in the medical journals.'

Helen and Jane went out of the hospital and across to the nurses' home, which was an attractive stone building with the same magnificent views of Hong Kong. Helen collected Jane's keys from reception and then took her along to a large bed-sitting room in the sister's wing. It had a small balcony which looked out over the bay, and the two of them went out to admire the view.

'It's fabulous at night-time,' said Helen. 'All the lights come on and you see them reflected in the water below. It's the most beautiful place on earth.'

The two of them stood there, looking far

below them at what appeared to be toy boats sailing over a glass pond. The air was pleasantly warm but not too hot now. They were absolutely quiet for a short time and then Jane took a deep breath and asked the question which was uppermost in her mind.

'Why does Dr Cynthia Martin still use her maiden name?'

'Well, it would be a bit confusing if she didn't, considering her husband is a doctor here too,' said Helen.

'Yes, of course.' Jane stood silently as the last of her newly-raised hopes shattered into a thousand pieces. She turned and went back into her room. 'I think I'll take Matron's advice and get some rest.'

'I think you should,' Helen said. 'You've had a long journey. If there's anything you need, I'm just along the corridor.'

'Thanks Helen,' Jane smiled. 'I just need some rest, that's all. I feel very tired.'

When Helen had gone, she took a shower and then lay down between the cool sheets of the narrow bed. She closed her eyes but, tired as she was, she couldn't sleep. After a while she drifted off and dozed for a few hours. When she awoke it was the middle of the night. From her bed she could see the moonlight shining through the windows. She got up and went out on to the balcony. Hong Kong was a vision of dazzling colour below her, full of life, a city that never seemed to sleep. On the hillsides there were twinkling lights in all the houses and the waterfront was a maze of flashing neon signs casting their glow on the water, where more sparkling lamps outlined the vessels which were resting there.

Jane caught her breath at the sheer beauty of it. She was once more in control of her life, a capable nursing sister, devoted and dedicated to her profession. The past was over; she was only concerned now with the present and the future. Closing the balcony windows, Jane went back to bed and slept soundly until morning.

CHAPTER TWO

THE HOT sun was shining through the windows when Jane awoke, feeling refreshed and ready for the day ahead. The jet lag, or whatever it was that had upset her, was completely gone and she leapt out of bed, anxious not to waste a second of the precious day. She flung wide the windows and stepped out on to the balcony. Far below, the busy city of Hong Kong was a hive of colourful activity and out on the bay the varied boats and ships were skimming along, miraculously avoiding collision. Jane took a deep breath; it felt good to be alive on a day like this, in such beautiful surroundings. There was a gentle tap on her door.

'Come in,' she called, and the door opened as Helen walked in.

'My, you look better! It's amazing what a good night's sleep will do. I've brought you a pot of tea,' she said, placing a tray on Jane's bedside table.

'Thanks very much.' Jane crossed the room and sank down on her bed. 'Will you stay and have a cup, Helen?'

'No thanks, I'm on duty in ten minutes. I just came to see if you want to go out to

Cheung Lau. Cynthia's going there to take the clinic this morning and she thought you might like to have a look round—that is, if you're fully recovered from yesterday.'

'Yes I'd love to,' said Jane eagerly.

'Well, you'll have to get your skates on, she's leaving in about half an hour. Nip down to the dining-room for a quick breakfast, then you'll find Cynthia out front. She's got a little yellow car—you can't miss it—we call it the yellow peril! I'll tell her you're coming. Bye for now,' and she was gone.

Jane gulped down the tea and pulled on a cool white cotton dress, suddenly remembering that she hadn't asked about uniform. Oh well, today she was still officially off duty, so it wouldn't matter. She grabbed her shoulder-bag and headed off down the corridor, hoping she was going in the direction of the dining-room. When she came to the end of the sister's wing she found a small sitting-room with easy chairs and soft cushions. There were books and magazines on small coffee-tables, but it certainly wasn't the dining-room!

A small blonde nurse was thumbing through a magazine. She looked up as Jane walked in and asked, 'Can I help you?'

Jane smiled at her. 'I'm Sister Marshall, I wonder if you could show me the way to the dining-room, Nurse?'

'Certainly, Sister.' The pretty nurse put her

magazine down and jumped to her feet. 'I'm Nicola Bryant and the dining-room's this way.'

Jane followed the young nurse along one of the corridors and down a small flight of stairs, and soon the delicious aroma of coffee told her that they were going in the right direction. They stopped outside the dining-room and the nurse held open the door.

'Here we are, Sister. I hope you enjoy your breakfast.' She smiled and ran lightly back up the stairs.

Jane went into the dining-room and chose a table by the window, so that she could see the view. There were very few people having breakfast, only a couple of doctors and one or two nurses. It looked as if the meal was nearly over. A young Chinese maid came over to her table and asked politely what she would like.

'Oh, something very light and very quick, please.' She added, smiling, 'I'm in a hurry. Just toast and coffee, I think—and do you have orange juice?'

'Yes, madam. We have eggs, bacon, sausage . . .'

'No thank you—just toast, coffee and orange juice will be fine.'

The maid went off and returned almost immediately with Jane's breakfast. Such efficiency! If this was typical of Hong Kong, she was certainly impressed.

Several minutes later Jane found herself

standing on the steps of the nurses' home. A small yellow sports car roared up almost immediately and screeched to a halt in front of her.

'Hi there!' called Cynthia. 'Glad you could make it. Hop in.' She pushed open the passenger door and Jane climbed in. The little yellow car seemed to take off like an aeroplane on a runway and Jane found herself holding her breath.

'Relax!' shouted Cynthia above the roar of the engine, 'I've never lost a passenger yet. I'm a good driver really, in spite of what my husband says.'

Jane forced herself to smile. 'He doesn't approve of your driving then?' she asked lightly.

'Oh, he's just a male chauvinist,' laughed Cynthia. 'Doesn't approve of the emancipation of women—can't think why he married a doctor.'

'But he still lets you go on working, I see,' said Jane.

'*Lets me!*' echoed Cynthia. 'Just let him try and stop me! Anyway, I only work part-time now, since the kids.'

'Oh, you have children then?'

'Yes, Jeremy's four and Rachael's two. A real handful they are—it's great to get away sometimes. Actually, they're adorable really, but I'm much better with other people's chil-

dren than my own.' She laughed her vivacious
laugh as she steered the car expertly round one
of the hairpin bends leading down into Hong
Kong. She slowed down slightly to allow for
the busy traffic as they got into the city centre,
but Jane was relieved when they reached the
waterfront and Cynthia stopped the car.

'OK, you can relax now,' said Cynthia,
sensing Jane's tension. 'The ordeal's over!'

Jane laughed, somewhat in relief. 'Oh, it
wasn't as bad as all that, I'm just a very
nervous passenger.'

'Well, that was obvious,' said Cynthia. 'I'll
slow down on the way back! Anyway, it's all
uphill, so I'll have to.'

They both laughed, but the atmosphere was
still a little strained. A young Chinese man had
come running out of one of the office-blocks
near the harbour as they arrived.

'Good-morning, Dr Martin,' he said
courteously.

'Ah, good-morning, Jo. This is Sister
Marshall.'

'Good-morning, Sister.' The young man
gave a slight bow and Jane smiled.

'Jo takes care of the hospital transport
arrangements for us—car parking, boat
maintenance and so forth. The hospital would
grind to a halt without him,' said Cynthia.

'Will you bring the car back about four
o'clock, Jo?'

'Certainly, Doctor,' Jo said efficiently as he took the keys from Cynthia. He climbed in and started the engine.

Cynthia turned back to Jane. 'I've got to be home by five today, so that I can spend some time with the family before I go out to Matron's dinner. Oh, I forgot to tell you about it. Matron asked me to invite you, if you'd fully recovered by this evening.'

'That will be nice,' Jane said as they walked along the waterfront.

'I should reserve judgment until afterwards,' laughed Cynthia. 'They can be a bit of a pain sometimes. She's a dear old soul, but a bit stiff and starchy. Not the sort of dinner where you can let your hair down. Here we are!' She stopped in front of a small motor launch.

'This is the hospital boat which takes us to the outlying islands. We've also got a helicopter, would you believe! Brand new it is— somebody has started pouring money into the hospital coffers, so things are looking up.'

They stepped aboard the motor launch and a young man came out of the cabin to greet them. 'Hello, Jim,' said Cynthia brightly.

'Good-morning, Doctor. Cheung Lau today?' he asked.

'Yes, that's right, whenever you're ready.'

The young man untied the moorings and started the engines. Soon he was easing the boat gently out of the congested harbour towards the wider expanse of the bay. The boat passed close to some quaint little wooden houses on stilts, built literally into the hillside, with their doorways almost in the water. Small children were playing outside the little houses and they waved and smiled as the boat went past. Jane and Cynthia waved back.

'*Wei!*' called Jane to the children in greeting.

'*Wei!*' they shouted back delightedly, and much more besides, which Jane could not understand. Cynthia smiled her approval. 'I see you've been doing your homework. Good for you—you'll need it when we're on Cheung Lau.'

'I'm not very good,' confessed Jane. 'But I did a crash course, and I never go anywhere without this.' She took her Cantonese phrase-book from her bag.

'Excellent,' said Cynthia. 'I've picked up quite a lot while we've been out here, so I'll help you if you get stuck. Mark is fluent of course—his family's been out here for years.'

'Yes, I suppose he would be,' said Jane quietly. Then, changing the subject quickly, she pointed to a nearby island.

'Where's that, Cynthia?' she asked, trying to sound interested.

'Oh, that's Green Island—obvious where it gets its name from, isn't it? I've never actually stopped off there, but it does look inviting, doesn't it? I'm always hurtling past on my way somewhere.'

'What's Cheung Lau like?' Jane asked.

'Oh, its a delightful island—you'll love it. Completely unspoiled—delightful beaches, lovely flowers, no cars,' she added laughingly.

'Now I *do* approve,' smiled Jane.

The boat continued its journey at a fairly leisurely pace and they had time to take in more of the exotic scenery—colourful boats of every description, small islands and the ever-glorious sunshine pouring down on the blue water.

'Mm, this is the life,' said Cynthia, closing her eyes as she sank into a deck-chair. 'Can't think why I go on working, on a day like this.'

'Probably because, like me, you enjoy your work,' said Jane cautiously. 'You're a career girl at heart.'

'Oh no I'm not!' Cynthia raised her hands in mock horror. 'I wouldn't change a thing! I love being married—and I love having children, even if they do drive me up the wall sometimes.' She laughed and added, 'I suppose I've got the best of both worlds, really.'

'Yes, I think you have,' Jane said quietly, gazing far out to sea. She concentrated all her attention on the horizon, hoping madly that the lump in her throat would disappear quickly, before she had to say something.

After a few seconds she cleared her throat and forced herself to speak.

'If Cheung Lau is an undeveloped island, why does it need a clinic?' she asked, relieved that her voice sounded quite normal.

'Oh, the clinic is not just for Cheung Lau. It's based there because that's where many of the fishing community settle for a while. They often stay in the harbour for a few weeks. We're trying to attract the attention of the boat people who would normally find it too difficult or too frightening to go to a big hospital. Word will soon get round that we're there, and then it's up to us to give them the best service we can.'

'I see.' Jane was thoughtful for a few seconds, then she asked, 'What sort of hours will the clinic be open?'

Cynthia laughed. 'That's up to you Jane. Theoretically, the clinic will be open every morning and you'll be in charge. A doctor will come out from St Margaret's twice a week, and also in an emergency if there's a case you can't handle. We've got our new helicopter, so it only takes a few minutes.'

'What about nursing staff?' asked Jane.

'You've got two excellent nurses. Both were born in Hong Kong but trained in the UK, so that's your language problem solved. Nurse Suzie Lee is about twenty-four I think, and male Nurse Chien Wong is in his late twenties.

They are both extremely well-trained and were selected from a large number of applicants. We had to be sure we'd chosen the right people. Mark interviewed them himself,' she added, 'so you can be sure they are of a high calibre.'

'Well, it all sounds very impressive,' Jane said. 'I must admit I had my qualms when I was first asked to come out here.'

'I'm sure you've no need to worry. I expect someone thought you were exactly the right person for the job,' said Cynthia, smiling reassuringly. 'Having met you, I approve of whoever was on the selection committee in the UK.'

'Thanks,' Jane said, thinking to herself that Cynthia was so much nicer than she had imagined her to be, all those years ago.

The boat was passing between several small islands and suddenly Cynthia called out, 'There it is! There's Cheung Lau.'

Jane looked in the direction she was pointing and saw a picturesque little island rising out of the water. The gentle slopes of its low hills were mostly green, with occasional patches of light brown earth where someone was making an attempt at cultivation. As they came into the harbour, their launch had to nose its way very gently through the tightly packed sampans, junks and fishing vessels. Washing-lines of multi-coloured garments flapped in the breeze and children played on the decks. A group of fishermen were mending their nets at the water's edge and Jim had to negotiate the launch expertly past them, so as not to become entangled. They looked up and called out.

'You see, they're already very friendly,' said Cynthia. 'It won't take much to win their confidence. They've already got used to seeing me here a few times, and several of them have already been round to the clinic.'

They got off the boat and started to walk through the market stalls clustered at the edge of the harbour. Most of them seemed to be selling fish, but there were a few others which contained a wide variety of goods, from shirts and shoes to cans of fizzy drinks and cigarettes.

Leaving the harbour, they walked through a narrow maze of streets and out into a grassy clearing at the foot of a small hill. The long, white building that was the clinic had been built in a square around a main compound, which was part garden, part waiting area. The waiting area had long, low benches shaded by trees, which had obviously been there before the clinic was built. A few people were sitting on the benches and they looked up in anticipation as Cynthia and Jane went into the clinic.

'We thought that initially we would have the waiting area outside, so that they don't actually have to commit themselves to walking through the door until someone comes out to escort them,' said Cynthia. 'It certainly seems to be working, although a few go away before we have time to see them. They're quite free to come inside if they wish, but most prefer to wait under the trees. This is the treatment room.'

They had walked through a reception area and were now in a large room with three cubicles, each of which could be curtained off when necessary. Each cubicle had an examination couch and at the side of the room were various trays and trolleys neatly set out.

'I usually see the patients in the reception area, and only bring them in here if I need to examine them. We've also got a small operating-theatre through there—for emergency use only, of course. Hopefully we shall be able to take our theatre cases over to St Margaret's by boat—or by helicopter if it's an emergency,' Cynthia elaborated.

The two clinic nurses had quietly come into the treatment room while Cynthia was showing Jane around and stood, uncertainly, waiting to be introduced. As soon as she noticed them Cynthia crossed the room to greet them.

'Ah, there you are, just in time to meet your new Sister. Suzie Lee, Chien Wong, this is Jane Marshall.'

Everyone shook hands and exchanged polite small talk about the weather and the beauty of the island, until Cynthia broke in.

'Well, let's get down to business. I'll take the clinic with Nurse Wong this morning. Nurse Lee, would you like to show Sister Marshall round the rest of the clinic? She's officially off duty until tomorrow, so we don't want to give her any work to do.'

'Oh, but I'd like to see what goes on here in the treatment room,' said Jane.

'Of course, but have a wander round first to get your bearings, and then come back here to meet the patients,' said Cynthia. 'Matter of fact, I might be quite glad of a little help at the end of the morning. I suddenly feel a bit tired and I've got a headache.'

She put her hand to her forehead. 'Strange! I *never* get headaches. Have we any aspirin in here?'

'Of course, Doctor.' Nurse Lee darted across to one of the cupboards and came back with the tablets and a glass of water.

'Hope I'm not sickening for something,' said Cynthia, gulping down the tablets. 'I'm usually as fit as a fiddle. Oh well, you run along and have a look around, Jane. I might have to ask you to take over later if I don't feel any better.'

'Sure, why not?' Jane said. 'Take it easy. I'll be back soon.'

She followed Nurse Lee out of the treatment room into the small operating-theatre. 'It's very simple, compared to the one at St Margaret's, but we could cope with minor

emergencies if we had to,' said Nurse Lee.
'And through here we have a recovery room
and three small sidewards, where patients can
stay when necessary. In theory, we shall try to
transfer them to St Margaret's whenever possible, but for minor illnesses or in cases where
they don't want to leave their relatives we shall
make use of these rooms.'

Jane opened the long windows of one of the
small sidewards and stepped out on to a
wooden veranda overlooking the garden.

'It's a delightful setting,' she said.

Nurse Lee followed her out. 'Yes, this
veranda runs all the way round the building, so
it's often quicker to go outside than walk
through the corridors. Come along, I'll show
you where we live.'

They walked along the veranda to the other
side of the building, which housed the nurses'
quarters.

'This is your room,' said Nurse Lee, walking
through the open windows and straight into a
neat little room, simply but adequately furnished. There was a bed covered with a pale
blue bedspread which matched the long, floor-
length curtains at either side of the windows.

'Everything was made on the island by local
craftsmen,' she explained, pointing out the
attractive bamboo armchair and dressing-
table.

'It's very pretty,' Jane said. 'I'm looking

forward to coming over here—tomorrow, I think.'

Nurse Lee smiled. 'We shall look forward to welcoming you, Sister. Now I'll show you our sitting-room.'

They went out on to the veranda again and past the other nurses' rooms to the little sitting-room which looked out towards the sea on one side and the hillside on the other.

'Sit down, Sister, we'll have some coffee,' Nurse Lee insisted. She went through into a small kitchen and spoke rapidly in Cantonese to someone there. A Chinese maid brought the coffee through and placed it on a small table, smiling at Jane as Nurse Lee introduced them. Jane understood very little of what was said, but gathered that she was being welcomed to Cheung Lau.

When the maid had gone Jane asked, 'What did you say her name was? It sounds quite unpronouncable!'

Nurse Lee laughed. 'It probably is, for you! Call her Mary—she'll be delighted. That's the nearest equivalent to her real name. She's absolutely marvellous , and she's an excellent cook. We've got a small dining-room through there. I hope you like Chinese food, by the way.'

'I know very little about it,' admitted Jane, 'but I'm willing to try anything.'

'Well, there are various kinds. I'll ask Mary

to go through her repertoire while you're here. How long will you be staying with us, Sister?'

'Just for the first six months; then I'm going back to St Catherine's,' said Jane. 'There's a hint of promotion in the air—something in administration, I think, but I'm not sure if I'll take it. I prefer to be working with the patients. Anyway, six months is a long time, and I've got to sort this job out first.' She added briskly, 'Shall we go and see how Dr Martin's getting along?'

They went out into the corridor and along to the treatment room. Nurse Wong had just finished putting sutures into a small laceration of the forearm. The patient, a young Chinese fisherman, was smiling happily and thanked Nurse Wong profusely as he went out.

'Where's Dr Martin?' Jane asked.

'She's out there in reception, but she's not very well. Her headache seems worse,' he said worriedly.

'Let's take a look.' Jane felt concerned. They went through into the reception area and found Cynthia slumped in an armchair, looking decidedly miserable.

'I feel awful,' she said. 'I think I must be going down with something. If it's all the same with you Jane, I think we'll head back to St Margaret's. There's nothing here that these nurses can't handle.'

Jane looked worried as she crossed the room

and started to take Cynthia's pulse. It was
much too rapid and her skin felt hot.

'Bring me a thermometer, Nurse Lee,' she
requested briskly.

'Oh, never mind all that rubbish,' said
Cynthia irritably. 'It's obvious I've got a
temperature! Just get me back to Hong Kong
so I can collapse at home.'

The journey back to Hong Kong seemed
interminable. Cynthia had started shivering
and was alternating between wrapping herself
in a blanket and then taking off as much
clothing as she could. At one point she did,
however, manage to say with a weak smile,
'They always say the medical profession make
the worst patients.'

Jane had telephoned ahead and Jo Chang
was at the quayside to meet them, with the
yellow sports car.

'Are you sure you can drive this thing?' he
asked Jane anxiously. Jane glanced at the com-
plicated dashboard and hesitated.

'Look, Sister, let me take Dr Martin home
in this, and I'll call a taxi to take you back to
hospital,' he said helpfully.

'That's an excellent idea. Thank you, Jo,'
Jane said, relieved. 'Cynthia, will you be all
right? Will someone be at home to meet you?'

'Stop fussing, woman,' muttered Cynthia.
'I've got a marvellous amah—she'll soon have
me tucked up in bed. Get yourself back to St

Margaret's. Oh, and don't forget Matron's dinner tonight. Don't expect I'll be there,' she added wryly.

Jane watched them drive off before stepping into the taxi which was waiting to drive her up the winding road. She looked out across the Hong Kong bay as they rose higher and higher up the hillside. It was strange how fond she had become of Cynthia in such a short time. Eight years ago she never thought she would have formed a friendship with Mark's wife.

Funny how things work out, she was musing to herself as she walked from the taxi across to the nurses' home. Pushing open the swing-doors she almost bumped into a tall, white-coated figure on his way out.

'Sorry,' they both said in unison, and then laughed as they recognised each other. Mark was the first to recover his composure.

'How are you settling in, Jane?' he asked.

'Oh, very well. I've just been across to Cheung Lau,' she answered, slightly breathlessly.

'And do you approve?' His voice was completely professional now. They were two strangers involved in the same medical project.

'I'm very impressed,' she said enthusiastically. 'I'm looking forward to going back there tomorrow to do some real work. I simply had a look around the place today. Cynthia's not very well,' she added quietly. 'She seems to be sickening for something, so she's gone home to bed.'

'Oh, really?' he said in a completely unconcerned voice. 'And what about you, are you fully recovered? Someone said you had a touch of jet lag last night. I hope we shall see you at Matron's dinner tonight.'

Jane was quite taken aback. She had just told him of his wife's illness and it hadn't affected him in the slightest!

'Yes, I shall be there,' she heard herself saying.

'Good,' he replied briskly. 'Until tonight then. Goodbye, Jane.'

Then he was gone, out through the swing-doors and striding across to the hospital in that self-assured way which she knew so well. She watched him enter and then went along to her room. Her pulse was racing. Perhaps I've caught Cynthia's fever, she thought. But no, it's not that . . .

This has got to stop, she told herself, furiously. Every time I see him I go back eight years in time. But he's a happily married man, with a splendid wife, who at this moment is suffering, and he doesn't seem to care—how callous of him! I'll go to Matron's dinner, but I'll make a point of avoiding Dr Mark Frobisher in the future . . .

CHAPTER THREE

JANE WAS choosing her dress for Matron's dinner very carefully. It had to be something chic and not too flamboyant. She was hoping to merge in with the crowd on this first social engagement in Hong Kong, to see how everyone behaved on such occasions. Her bedside telephone shrilled and Jane picked it up.

'Sister Marshall here. Oh, Matron, how nice of you to call. Yes, I'm looking forward to it immensely.'

Matron's lilting voice was now asking about Jane's visit to Cheung Lau.

'Very impressive, Matron. I'm certainly looking forward to my work there. Oh, did anyone tell you that Dr Martin is unwell?'

'Yes, her amah telephoned me, so I went round to see her and to make sure all was well.'

How typical of Matron to find the time to visit Cynthia, even though she was preparing a dinner party, thought Jane.

'And how is she?' she asked.

'I think she's got this forty-eight hour flu that's going around. I hope you don't get it. It can be quite debilitating. You must let me know if you notice you have any of the signs and symptoms.'

'Of course, Matron,' soothed Jane. 'I feel very well at the moment.'

'Good, good.' Her voice droned on reassuringly. 'Well, we'll see you in a few minutes then. Goodbye, Sister.'

'Goodbye, Matron.' Jane put the phone down and smiled to herself. What a dear old soul Matron is, she thought. I wonder if I shall finish up like her—giving advice to all the young medical staff!

She returned to the problem of which dress to wear. Yes, the pure silk one, slim-fitting but not too tight. It had an attractive boat-shaped neckline which was not too low-cut. She tried it on and looked at her reflection in the long mirror. Yes, eminently suitable. She applied a touch of makeup—not too much—and as she stepped into strappy high heels she felt that her appearance was just right. She was completely composed and ready to enjoy the evening— just so long as she didn't have to talk to Mark.

The evening air was pleasantly cool as Jane walked across the nurses' home garden to Matron's little house. It was set back from the rest of the buildings and looked welcoming, even from the outside. Someone—probably Matron—had cultivated roses around the porch, and there were exotic plants and shrubs in large earthenware pots standing on either side.

The door was open and the sound of voices and laughter floated out into the night. Jane walked cautiously inside and joined the throng of doctors and nurses who were chattering away to each other about every subject under the sun. It seemed obvious to Jane that off-duty medical staff at St Margaret's were quite definitely *off duty*. They were meant to enjoy themselves, to relax, and to forget the cares and worries of the hospital. This was how they recharged their batteries for the work ahead, and it simply wasn't done to talk shop. Matron spotted Jane almost immediately and bore down upon her with a welcoming smile.

'How charming you look, Sister. Welcome to my little house! What will you have to drink?'

Jane glanced nervously around her before replying, 'A gin and tonic, please.'

Matron beckoned to one of the servants. 'A gin and tonic for Sister Marshall, please.' She turned back to Jane. 'Now come and meet some of my guests. Sister Benson you've met, haven't you?'

The two sisters smiled at each other as Matron carried on with her introductions, raising her voice to attract attention.

'This is Sister Marshall everybody; I hope

you'll all introduce yourselves and make her feel welcome.'

All eyes seemed to be on Jane. A pleasant, athletic-looking doctor of about thirty stepped forward and held out his hand to her.

'I'm Martin Chandler,' he said, smiling appraisingly at her as they shook hands. 'I heard there was an attractive addition to our little community, but I didn't know quite how attractive until this moment.'

Jane smiled. 'I bet you say that to all the girls,' she laughed.

'Only to the pretty ones,' he countered in a bantering tone. 'Have you got a drink?'

'It's coming I think—yes, here it is.' The servant had arrived with an ice-cold gin and tonic, and Jane took a grateful sip, then a little more. She began to mellow towards her good-humoured companion.

'How long are you staying out here?' he asked.

'About six months—until the Cheung Lau project is established,' she replied.

'Then we'll have to make the most of your time with us,' he smiled. 'You must let me show you round the Hong Kong night-spots sometime. They're absolutely unique—not to be missed.'

'Sounds fun! Yes, I'd like that,' Jane said with guarded interest.

'Well, when are you off duty?' he persisted.

'Hold on a minute,' she laughed, 'I've only just arrived! Give me time to settle in. To-morrow I'm going out to Cheung Lau, so we'll have to see how things go after that.'

'I'll hold you to it,' he said sternly.

'I'm sure you will!'

Matron was beginning to lead her guests through into the dining-room, so Jane followed, Dr Chandler still at her side.

'Sister Marshall?' Matron called out. 'Ah, there you are. Come over here. I've put you next to Dr Frobisher so that you can talk about old times together.'

Jane froze and the room seemed to go very quiet all of a sudden. Matron was beckoning her and, as if in a dream, she found herself drifting obediently across to her allotted place. Mark was standing by the side of her chair.

'Do sit down, my dear,' Matron instructed as she hurried off to show her other guests where to sit.

Mark pulled Jane's chair away from the table and then courteously pushed it under as she sat down. She was seething inside; the last thing she wanted to talk about was *old times*, and the last person she wanted to talk to was Dr Frobisher. Why wasn't he at home looking after his sick wife? She picked up the crisp, white napkin and laid it firmly on her lap. If anyone was to do the talking it wasn't going to be her.

Suddenly she was aware of another figure sitting down on her other side. It was her new friend, Martin Chandler.

'Thought I'd lost you just now,' he said with an infectious grin, adding in a whisper, 'I had to talk Matron into switching a few places around! Caused her no end of a flap, poor soul. She's a bit set in her ways.'

'So I've noticed,' laughed Jane, relieved to find Martin next to her. Mark, sitting on her other side, waited for a suitable moment to attract her attention.

As she turned her head slightly towards him he said, 'I wonder which particular old times Matron thought we should like to talk about?' His piercing blue eyes were smiling at her in the way that had always made her want to melt into his arms. Jane forced herself to remain detached. This is just another married man whom I knew a long time ago, she told herself.

'I don't remember very much about them,' she said in a cold voice. 'I prefer to live in the present, myself.'

The blue eyes flickered for an instant; Mark had lost some of his composure, but he soon recovered. He gave Jane a polite smile and turned away to talk to Sister Benson, who was sitting on the other side of him.

'So you and Mark were at the same hospital?' said Martin, seemingly unaware of the tension between them.

'Yes, but it's all a long time ago. We'd quite forgotten each other,' said Jane lightly. Quickly changing the subject, she added, 'I wonder what's on the menu tonight? I notice we've all got chopsticks.'

'Oh, Matron insists on being authentic. When in Rome, as they say. At St Margaret's you've got to be able to use chopsticks as well as you can use forceps. Matron gives you a test before you leave here. Honestly,' he added because Jane was laughing so much at him.

'Pull the other one!' she sputtered. 'Seriously though, you'll have to show me what to do with these things.'

'Well, it's very simple,' he said helpfully. 'You hold this one firmly like that—this one doesn't move, it's like an anchor—and then the other one is placed here . . . and that's the one that does all the work. You'll soon get the hang of it.'

'I hope so—wouldn't want to fail the end of term chopstick test,' said Jane gaily, and they both giggled in a conspiratorial way. Jane was aware that Mark was watching them now, but she ignored him completely. Large bowls of soup were being placed on the table and everyone had started to help themselves.

'Shark's-fin soup,' said Matron.

'My favourite. It's delicious but frightfully expensive. I don't know how Matron can afford it—she must have private means! I bet she's got an enormous castle back on the Emerald Isle. Here, let me help you.' Martin spooned some of the soup into Jane's bowl.

'Not too much,' she protested. 'I don't know if I shall like it. It looks a bit slimy.'

'Slimy?' he echoed in mock horror. Then, leaning across her, he said, 'Mark, did you hear this young lady call shark's fin soup *slimy*?'

Mark seemed pleased to be included in the conversation again.

'Wait till you taste it Jane. I'm sure you'll like it,' he said smoothly.

Jane took a sip and agreed. 'Mm . . . it's delicious.'

'Would you like some more?' Mark asked, reaching for the large bowl.

'No thank you,' Jane said firmly. More food was being brought in by the servants, and she tried a crispy pancake served with shallots and a sweet red paste. Next came a delicious dish of Peking duck, some dishes of vegetables and rice and a variety of other different kinds of meat, all garnished in a most decorative way. Everyone helped themselves from the dishes in the centre of the table. Jane noticed that most of the guests seemed to manipulate their chopsticks expertly, so she struggled on. Practice makes perfect, she told herself. The servants continually replenished the delicate china teacups with refreshing jasmine tea.

Mark made another attempt at conversation towards the end of dinner. Jane was coolly polite but, true to her intention, she tried her utmost to discourage him. He seemed outwardly composed and self-assured; only his eyes betrayed the fact that he was hurt by her attitude.

After dinner, coffee was served on the balcony and the conversation initially centred around the amazing view of the lights of Hong Kong. Even at night-time it was possible to distinguish various well-known landmarks by the flashing neon signs and the glittering street lights. Martin pointed out some of his favourite restaurants to Jane.

'You must let me take you out to dinner as soon as you're free,' he was saying. Mark had now left the pair of them together and was talking to Nicola Bryant, the pretty little blonde nurse who had shown Jane the way to the dining-room that morning. They seemed entirely engrossed in their conversation, but once, as Jane looked in their direction, Mark also glanced across, and their eyes met for a brief second. Hurriedly Jane turned her attention back to Martin, just as a servant came out on to the balcony and whispered something to Matron.

'Dr Chandler, you're wanted in casualty, I'm afraid,' called Matron.

'Duty calls,' he sighed to Jane. 'I'll give you

a ring at the clinic in a day or two, and perhaps we can arrange a night on the town.'

Jane smiled. 'That would be lovely. I'll look forward to it.' And what was more, she meant it.

When he had gone Jane mingled with the other guests, trying to remember as many new names as possible. Little by little the party seemed to be breaking up. The night air resounded with profuse thanks for the splendid dinner as people drifted away. Jane was still standing at the edge of the balcony, leaning against the rails, absorbed in the beautiful view. She turned at last to go inside and suddenly a hand was on her arm, a strong familiar hand.

This was the first time Mark had touched her for eight years, but still she shivered involuntarily. She looked up into the blue eyes of the man she had once loved so much and saw the hurt expression on his face. What was even more disconcerting was the fact that everyone else had gone inside; they were alone, in the moonlight, on the balcony. Another time, long, long ago, another place, now far away, and Jane would have melted into Mark's arms. But there was no possibility of that now.

'Jane, I must talk to you,' he said, moving closer. 'I realise that you've changed in eight years, but why do you hate me so much?'

'I think hate is rather a strong word,' she said coldly. 'I would simply prefer to keep our friendship on a professional basis.'

'Well, that will do for a start, I suppose,' he said quietly, moving closer. She tried to move away, but suddenly his arms were round her, his hard body pressed against hers. She lifted her eyes to his face to remonstrate, but instead found herself responding to his long, lingering kiss. She closed her eyes and for a few brief seconds forgot the intervening years. They were both young and in love for the first time . . .

'No!' Jane pulled herself away, remembering the impossibility of the situation. She turned and ran back into the house. Matron was saying goodbye to the last of her guests as Jane arrived breathlessly at the front door. Mark was following closely behind her.

'Thank you for a lovely evening, Matron,' he said in a composed, professional voice, which gave no hint of the turmoil of the last few seconds.

'Yes, it was most enjoyable,' Jane added. 'Thank you, Matron.'

'It was a pleasure,' said Matron, as Jane and Mark stepped out into the warm, Hong Kong night. Jane quickened her step and, as soon as they were out of earshot, turned to Mark and spoke in a cold voice.

'As I was saying, our relationship must be

purely professional. You must surely realise that, Mark.'

'But, Jane, we had something very special between us. How can you . . .'

'How can *I*? How can *I*?' she interrupted furiously. 'You've got a nerve, Mark Frobisher!' Angrily she turned and ran into the nurses' home and along the corridor. As she turned to go into the sister's wing she came face to face with Nicola Bryant who stared in amazement at the tears in Jane's eyes.

'Goodnight, Sister,' she said softly, and watched as Jane retreated into the safety of her room.

'Goodnight, Nurse Bryant,' said Jane in a firm voice which sounded far away, and not at all like her own.

That's all I need, she thought as she closed the door. I don't want rumours to start spreading round the hospital. She sat down at the dressing-table and dabbed her eyes. Tomorrow I'll be on Cheung Lau, far away from temptation. I can get on with the job I came out to do and leave Mark Frobisher to his responsibilities here. With any luck we won't have to meet very often. She closed her eyes as the tears once more sprang up in them and flowed down her cheeks.

CHAPTER FOUR

THE SEA was calm and blue as the hospital launch surged forward towards Cheung Lau. Jane had deliberately put the events of the previous evening from her mind and was concentrating her full attention on the work ahead. She had several ideas she wanted to put into practice as soon as possible, but she was prepared to go along with the existing policy to start with. The colourful boats of the harbour came into view and Jim was soon helping her on to the shore. He picked up her heavy suitcase and walked beside her.

'*Ng Goi*,' she said to him with a smile.

He replied, in English, 'I think Sister will soon speak our language very well.'

'I hope so,' Jane laughed.

She looked at the front of the clinic and saw that things were much busier than the previous day. There was a queue of patients waiting outside under the trees, and some had actually ventured into the reception area and were sitting around on the bamboo chairs. There was no sign of either of the nurses.

Really, this is too bad, was Jane's immediate reaction. Now that we've attracted the atten-

tion of the boat people, the least we can do is
give them a proper medical service. She strode
purposefully through into the treatment
room—there was no one there. Jane was beginning to feel decidedly anxious as she went
out on to the veranda and round to the other
side of the building. Then, through the open
windows of one of the little side wards, she saw
both Nurse Lee and Nurse Wong attending to
a young woman patient. Jane entered the
room, and the first thing she noticed was a tiny
new-born baby in a cot at the foot of the bed.
The baby was sleeping peacefully and the
mother lying in the bed, although looking
tired, seemed fairly comfortable.

'When did this happen?' she asked.

'During the night,' said Nurse Lee. 'She
arrived at the clinic in the final stages of
labour, so we had to admit her at once.'

'It was a breech birth,' added Nurse Wong.

'It was a *breech* birth?' echoed Jane. 'And
you delivered her yourselves? Why didn't you
ring St Margaret's?'

The male nurse shrugged his shoulders.
'What good would it have done? By the time
one of the doctors had got out here it would
have been too late.'

'You were very lucky,' Jane said, in a severe
tone. 'In future I want you to ring for a doctor immediately, as soon as an emergency
arises.'

'I've delivered a breech baby before,' said Nurse Lee defensively.

'That's not the point,' retorted Jane starchily. 'The policy is that we inform the doctor in charge and he can then decide on the best course of action.'

'I think you would have done what we did, if you'd been here, Sister,' said Nurse Wong quietly. 'We really had no choice except to get on with it.'

'Very well,' Jane said, slightly mollified. 'I'm relieved that mother and baby appear to be thriving. Are there any post-natal complications?'

'Nothing serious, Sister,' said Nurse Lee. 'I had to put in a couple of sutures after the birth, but otherwise she seems healthy—she's very young, of course.' She spoke rapidly in Cantonese to the young woman and then smiled at the reply.

'Yes, she's only sixteen, Sister. It was her mother who brought her in last night.'

'Well, we've been very lucky,' Jane conceded. 'I feel very thankful that the pair of you were able to cope so well. Now, what about all those outpatients? Couldn't one of you have started the morning clinic?'

'I started the clinic at eight o'clock,' said Nurse Wong patiently, 'and admitted the first two patients.'

'Admitted them? But that means all our

in-patient beds are now full!' Jane exclaimed. 'Did you *have* to admit them?'

'Yes, they both require hospitalisation,' the male nurse continued in a quiet, professional voice. 'Come and see for yourself.'

He led the way through to the next room where an old man was propped on pillows and wearing an oxygen mask. His face was grey, his nose pinched and drawn, and he was breathing with difficulty. Also in the tiny room were two young men—obviously sons of the patient—and an old lady, tearfully sitting beside her husband.

'I see what you mean,' said Jane quietly, moving towards the patient so that she could feel the feeble pulse.

'The sons carried him in soon after he'd collapsed,' said Nurse Wong. 'I examined him and diagnosed coronary thrombosis. He's too weak to be moved, and anyway the relatives don't want him to leave the island.'

Jane smiled reassuringly at the relatives. 'Tell them we shall do all we can,' she said to Nurse Wong, who rapidly translated the message. The old lady smiled through her tears and one of her sons put his arm round her.

They went towards the third room. Nurse Wong paused outside the door.

'Let me tell you about this patient, Sister. She speaks some English so I don't want to explain the details in front of her. When she arrived at the clinic this morning it was simply to ask for some cough medicine. She was chain-smoking as she sat outside waiting and didn't like it when we asked her to put her cigarette out when she got inside the treatment room. During a routine examination of the chest, Nurse Lee detected a lump in the patient's left breast. Apparently it's been there for some time and it's going to need surgery—a biopsy at the very least,' he added.

'But why admit her here? Why not send her to St Margaret's?' asked Jane.

'Because it's the only way I could keep an eye on her. She's very scared of big hospitals and it's going to take someone very persuasive to get her up to St Margaret's. Besides, her chest is in a terrible state—she must have been smoking since she was a child. We'll have to clear up the bronchitis before anyone can operate.'

Jane went in to see the patient and examined the lump in her breast, noting the frightened look in the woman's eyes as she did so.

'Don't worry,' she said patting the patient's hand. 'We'll look after you. You're quite safe here.'

'I want a cigarette,' said the young woman.

'No, I'm afraid you can't have one. They're very bad for your chest,' said Jane quietly.

'I *must* have a cigarette,' repeated the patient desperately.

Nurse Wong intervened and spoke rapidly in Cantonese. The young woman frowned and sank back sulkily on her pillows.

'I'll come back to see you when we've finished the morning clinic,' said Jane, smiling her most professional smile. The patient scowled back at her and Jane beat a hasty retreat.

Outside the door she turned to Nurse Wong. 'You were quite right to admit her. I only hope Dr Frobisher approves of all this. You have rung him, I suppose?'

Nurse Wong hesitated before he replied. 'Sister, we've been so busy, we haven't had time. I was going to ring him later this morning.'

'Nurse Wong, you *must* notify the doctor in charge as soon as you admit a patient,' lectured Jane. 'Look, ask Nurse Lee to take care of the in-patients until the doctor arrives, and you and I will deal with the out-patients.'

Jane went briskly along to the reception area and smiled reassuringly at the people who were drifting in to see what was holding up the proceedings. There was a tiny office by the front door where Jane remembered seeing a phone. She picked it up and dialled St Margaret's.

'I'd like to speak to Dr Frobisher,' she told the receptionist who answered. 'This is Sister Marshall at the Cheung Lau clinic.'

There was a pause of several seconds and then a deep, professional voice came over the phone. 'Dr Frobisher here.'

'Mark, this is Jane,' she said quickly.

'Good-morning Sister Marshall,' came the curt reply.

'Oh, good-morning,' said Jane, hardly recognising the cold voice at the other end. She adjusted her manner accordingly. 'I'm notifying you that we've admitted three patients whom I think you should see as soon as possible.' Her voice was cool and impersonal. She waited for his reply but several seconds elapsed in silence.

'Are you still there, Dr Frobisher?' she asked.

'Yes, I'm still here.' The voice was ominously calm. 'I'm wondering why you are notifying me of three admissions all at the same time. You realise that the clinic is now full, Sister?'

'Yes, Doctor. The patients had all been admitted before I arrived this morning and . . .'

'Don't make excuses, Sister,' he snapped. 'You are in charge of the nursing staff. You take ultimate responsibility for their actions.'

'Of course,' said Jane. 'But there were extenuating circumstances in all three cases— they *had* to be admitted. Personally, I think you will find that the in-patient accommodation will have to be extended, once the project gets under way.'

'We are not interested in your personal opinion, Sister,' he retorted sharply. 'It is your professional skill which is of paramount importance.'

Jane stared in disbelief at the phone in her hand. Could this possibly be the warm, emotional man she had been with yesterday evening? Well, she thought, I did ask for a professional relationship. But I hadn't expected anything quite like this!

'Would you give me your provisional diagnoses of the three patients, Sister.'

'Certainly; we have a breech-birth mother and baby, a coronary thrombosis and a suspected breast cancer,' Jane said briskly. 'How soon can you make it over here, Doctor?'

'I shall send Dr Chandler. I have to be in surgery for the rest of the morning, and these aren't exactly emergencies, are they? He'll be with you in a couple of hours.'

There was a click and the phone went dead. Jane carefully replaced the receiver and stared out of the window, numb with shock. Then she remembered the waiting patients and walked back into the reception area. Nurse Wong was already talking to an old man, and he brought him over to Jane's desk. She sat down and devoted her full attention to the patient in front of her.

Jane and Nurse Wong managed to attend to several patients, and fortunately no one had needed admission to the already full clinic, by the time the athletic figure of Martin Chandler, surgical bag in hand, came jauntily across the compound. Jane spotted him through the window and he saw her and waved. She waved back and the tension of the last hour disappeared. She turned to Nurse Wong.

'Will you carry on here, please? I'm going to take Dr Chandler to see the new patients.'

Martin came into the reception area, beaming all over his good-humoured face.

'Whatever did you say to the boss this morning?' he asked Jane. 'Oh boy, was he in a foul mood!'

'I simply notified him of three admissions,' Jane said quietly.

'Well, he certainly over-reacted then,' said Martin, with a smile. 'Lead me to them, Sister, and let's get on with some work. The coronary first.'

They went in to see Mr Kwan, the coronary patient. Martin asked the relatives if they would wait outside while he made a full examination and gave an injection. Then he turned to Jane.

'I think we'll keep him here—no point trying to move him to St Margaret's, it would only distress the relatives. Keep him on the oxygen for the moment until his colour and breathing improves. We'll start him on medication now and do some tests when he's a bit stronger. Nurse Lee, would you let his family know what's happening?'

The next visit was to the young mother and baby. Martin examined them and approved of the treatment so far.

'She wants to go home Doctor,' said Nurse Lee. 'Says her mother needs help with the washing.'

'Well, her mother'll have to wait,' said Martin firmly. 'She needs a few days rest, at the very least. See if you can feed her up a bit—she's very skinny. She'll need to be strong to feed the baby and do all the other work expected of her. Poor little mite.' He smiled at the patient and spoke a few words in halting Cantonese. She smiled and nodded back at him.

'That's OK then. She'll stay for a while. Fatten her up, if you can—high-protein diet, and lots of milk if she'll drink it.' He turned his attention to the baby and tickled him gently under the chin. 'I bet you'll drink your fair share, won't you? Nothing wrong with you.'

Martin and Jane went into the next room, but it was completely empty. Through the open windows they could see their patient sitting on the ground, in the shade of a tree, and pulling hard on a cigarette, pausing only to give an occasional racking cough. Martin strode angrily out into the garden.

Whatever it was he said to her, it made her jump to her feet and run back into the room, dropping her cigarette as she went. Jane held back the covers and she climbed into the bed, completely subdued. Martin examined her chest, then the lump in her breast, after which he told her he would wash his hands of her if she didn't do as she was told. She nodded obediently and lay very still when Jane and Martin left her.

'You were a bit harsh with her, weren't you?' Jane said, once they were outside the door.

'Had to be cruel to be kind,' he shrugged. 'We've got to clear up that chest as soon as we can, so that we can operate on the breast.' He scribbled something on her notes. 'I've written her up for penicillin—make sure she gets it. I'd like her in surgery within a week, if possible. The longer we leave that lump, the worse things will be. It could be benign, of course, but we shan't know until we've done a biopsy.'

They went back into the reception area and spent the rest of the morning dealing with the out-patients. It was after two o'clock before they finally closed the front door of the clinic and made their way to the little dining-room at the back of the building. Mary was hovering in the background with the lunch she had prepared an hour ago. Good-tempered as always, she smiled as the doctor and staff came in, and showed them to their table. It was a superb meal based on a variety of seafood.

'I hope you like fish,' whispered Martin in Jane's ear. 'Because there's plenty of it around Cheung Lau and it's always fresh.'

Mary placed the dishes on the table and then went back into the kitchen, still smiling. Jane picked up her chopsticks, and found that her skill with them had definitely improved.

'I'm very impressed,' said Martin. 'Such dexterity, Sister! You should have been a surgeon.' At this point Jane inadvertently dropped a king-prawn, which she was in the act of negotiating from the main serving dish to her own plate, on to the white table-cloth. They all laughed.

'Martin, you shouldn't say things like that— it's just tempting fate,' she protestd.

'Is it?' he said softly. She glanced at the earnest expression on his usually whimsical face and looked away again, concentrating her attention on the chopsticks.

After lunch Martin said he had to get back to St Margaret's. Nurse Wong said he would look after the in-patients during the afternoon so that Nurse Lee could help Jane settle in to her new quarters.

'That's very gallant of you,' said Martin to

the male nurse. 'That means Sister can see me back to the launch.'

Jane looked up. 'Why, of course, Martin. I'll be back in a minute,' she said to Nurse Lee.

Martin took hold of Jane's arm and steered her out into the warm sunlight.

'What a wonderful island this is,' he said. 'I envy you being out here—I shall make a point of coming over as often as possible, and not just for the scenery, either. Still, you'll need to get away once in a while. How about Saturday night? Can you fix some off duty time?'

'Well, I don't know. I haven't got around to sorting that out yet. I want to be fair to the others,' said Jane.

'Of course you do. Well, sort it out and let me know. You could come over in the early evening. I'll meet you in Hong Kong and show you round the night spots. We could stay out all night if you like—Hong Kong never sleeps. Or you could ask Matron for a room at St Margaret's,' he added, seeing the look on her face.

'If I can make it, I'll book a room at St Margaret's,' said Jane with a smile. 'Goodbye then. I'll let you know.'

'Goodbye,' he said, and to her surprise he bent down and kissed her briefly on the cheek. She turned quickly and walked back into the clinic.

Nurse Lee was waiting to show her to her

room and help her unpack. When they had finished they went along to the sitting-room and joined Nurse Wong for some tea.

'I think I'll keep the off-duty times fairly flexible,' said Jane cautiously. 'Let me know when you need time off and we'll fix it between us. So long as we cover the work and everyone does their fair share, that's the main thing.'

Both nurses agreed, so she continued, 'I'd like to take Saturday night off, if both of you are available here.'

'That's fine by me,' said Nurse Wong.

Nurse Lee smiled, 'Of course, Sister.' Then she added shyly, 'Are you going to see Hong Kong by night?'

'Yes, I hope so,' said Jane.

'You'll love it,' Nurse Lee said enthusiastically. 'No city in the world is quite like Hong Kong.'

'I'm beginning to think so myself,' agreed Jane. She was certainly looking forward to her night on the town.

CHAPTER FIVE

JANE did an early-morning round of her three in-patients to check that all was well before she started the out-patient clinic. She had a long chat with the young woman with the bad chest, who turned out to speak quite good English.

'Call me Carol,' she said to Jane. 'That's a nice English name, and it sounds like my own. I went to school many times, but my mother and father were always moving along. I can write though, and I like to read.'

'Where do you live now?' asked Jane, pleased that her patient was showing a more friendly attitude.

The young woman shrugged her shoulders. 'Wherever I find myself,' she said. 'Sometimes on the islands, sometimes Hong Kong. I go wherever I feel like it. I don't like to stay in one place too long.' She smiled at Jane and then asked quietly, 'Any chance of a cigarette, Sister?'

'Carol, I've told you about the dangers of cigarettes. With a chest like yours it would be suicidal to smoke now,' Jane said firmly. 'Besides, we've got to get you better for next

70

week. You're going to need an operation to check on that lump in your breast.'

Carol lay very still and quiet in the bed; then she looked at Jane with imploring eyes. 'Tell me Sister, what are my chances?'

'First we shall do a a biopsy, to determine the nature of the lump,' Jane said in a calm voice. 'The sooner we can do that the better, so remember—*no* cigarettes, Carol.'

'OK, Sister.' She gave a pathetic little cough and Jane patted her hand.

'Just be a good girl and we'll do all we can for you,' Jane said as she went out, closing the door quietly behind her. Oh dear, she thought. I'm beginning to sound just like Matron! Another twenty years and everyone will think me a dear old soul . . .

She went in to see Mr Kwan. He was breathing much more easily. Nurse Lee had removed the oxygen mask and was giving him a wash.

'My, you're looking better today,' said Jane, smiling at the old man. Then, remembering he couldn't understand her, she tried, in halting Cantonese, to find out how he was feeling. The old man looked enquiringly at her.

'He's a bit deaf,' said Nurse Lee helpfully.

'I don't think he understands my atrocious accent,' said Jane with a smile. 'I'll have to work on it. Ask him how he's feeling, Nurse Lee.'

There followed a long dialogue, some of which Jane found she could understand. 'He's a little better, but still feels tired, doesn't he?' Jane said to Nurse Lee.

'Well done, Sister!' said Nurse Lee. 'He's a much better colour today, too.'

'Yes. We'll discontinue the oxygen,' said Jane. 'But keep the mask near the bed, just in case.'

She helped Nurse Lee to make the old man comfortable on his pillows, and then they went in to see the young mother and her baby. 'Any problems here, Nurse?' asked Jane.

'No Sister. The baby's thriving, but I think the mother needs lots of rest. She's not very strong.'

'You're right about that,' said Jane, looking at the skinny young girl lying back on her pillows.

'She says she ought to get back to her family,' said Nurse Lee.

'Out of the question,' Jane said firmly. 'We'll find some way of keeping her here for a few days. She needs looking after. Baby feeding all right?'

'Round the clock, if he can get it,' smiled Nurse Lee. 'No problem there.' The baby had started to cry lustily, and the mother was holding her arms out for him.

'There, what did I tell you?' Nurse Lee laughed. 'He's hungry again. I'm trying to get him into a routine, but his mother thinks otherwise.'

Jane smiled. 'I suppose he'll get fed on demand when he's at home, so there's no point starting him off differently here. The only thing is, it's a bit wearying for his poor little mum. Well, I'm off to see the out-patients. Nurse Wong is going to help me, so will you hold the fort at this end, please?'

'Certainly, Sister.' Nurse Lee picked up the howling baby and handed him to his mother.

Jane went across to the reception area where Nurse Wong was already seeing the first patient. There were only ten patients that morning and all were minor cases which could be treated on the spot. Jane asked two of the ante-natal patients, who were making their first visit to the clinic, to return the next day so that the doctor could see them. She found herself wondering which doctor it would be. Martin had made the last visit and Cynthia was still off sick. I suppose it will be Mark, she thought with a shiver.

Sure enough, at nine o'clock exactly the next day, Dr Mark Frobisher marched briskly through the front door of the reception area. Jane looked up from her desk, where she was completing her report.

'Good-morning, Sister,' he said in a completely neutral voice. 'Are you aware that there are two very pregnant young ladies sitting outside in the hot sun?'

'They're waiting to see *you*, Dr Frobisher,' Jane answered, as politely as she could.

'Indeed? Well, don't you think they would be more comfortable inside?' he asked. The blue eyes were cold and hostile as he glared down at her.

'I've already invited them in,' Jane said acidly, 'but they prefer to sit outside—it's quite cool under the trees.' She moved away from her desk. 'Would you like me to bring them in now, Doctor?'

'Of course, Sister.' He turned and went into the treatment room.

Jane went out into the hot sunlight. Really, this is becoming intolerable, she thought. Surely we can find a compromise between wild passion and open hostility? She smiled as she beckoned to the two young women. As she watched them waddling towards her, she instinctively knew that Mark would not be pleased that this was their first ante-natal examination. One of them looks about six months pregnant, and the other must be almost full-term, she thought. She led them through into the treatment room where Mark was waiting.

It took several minutes to prepare the two patients for examination; Jane knew that Mark was becoming impatient as he waited outside the curtained cubicles. She could hear his footsteps, pacing up and down the room.

'We're ready now, Doctor,' she called, in a deliberately sweet voice.

He pulled back the curtain and came into the cubicle of the first patient.

'Kindly see that the patients are prepared before I arrive next time, Sister,' he said coldly.

'Oh, I will, Doctor,' Jane smiled sarcastically. 'I'm sorry to keep you waiting.'

He turned his attention to the patient, and his manner changed. He devoted himself entirely to the task in hand and Jane found herself admiring his professional skill, in spite of herself. He's a brilliant doctor, she thought. Always was—always will be.

There were no complications, fortunately, so when Mark had finished his examinations they went back into the reception area. Mark had lost some of his brusque attitude during his concentration on the patients.

'I do wish these young girls would seek medical help at the beginning of their pregnancy,' he complained to Jane.

'Perhaps they will, when they get used to the fact that we're here,' she said, sitting down at her desk. 'Would you like a coffee, Doctor?'

'Thank you, Sister, I would.' His eyes flickered for an instant before he turned to look at the waiting patients. 'In about half an hour, I think,' he added. 'I'd better see some of the patients first.'

There was an uneasy truce between them, and Jane hoped they could keep it that way. When they took a coffee-break together in the small sitting-room, they were like two polite medical colleagues, discussing their patients. Mark asked endless questions about the in-patients and then said he would like to see them. He completed a full examination of each one before returning to finish the out-patient session.

'Will you stay to lunch, Doctor?' asked Jane at the end of the morning. 'We have an excellent cook here.'

For an instant Mark hesitated. He seemed on the point of accepting her offer—and then, as if remembering something, he shook his head. 'No, thank you, Sister,' he said firmly. Then picking up his medical bag he strode towards the front door. Jane was left standing in the middle of the reception area, feeling as if she had been swept around by a tornado.

She tidied her desk automatically, putting away the case notes in the filing cabinet and arranging her papers in the appropriate drawers. This is how it's got to be, she thought. This is the only relationship we can possibly have—but just to be near him is agony some-times. To watch those sensitive hands, skilfully examining a patient, to see those blue eyes looking into mine . . . She slammed a drawer shut, took a deep breath and walked briskly along to the dining-room.

Nurse Wong was sitting at the table and Mary was waiting to serve the lunch. Jane flashed them both a brilliant smile and sat down, prepared to enjoy the delicious dishes which Mary was already placing in front of her. Nurse Lee was, of course, still with the patients.

'Today we are having *Dim Sum*,' said Nurse Wong.

'It looks delightful,' said Jane, admiring the small, round bamboo baskets of food. 'But what is it?'

'You must try a little of everything,' he told her. 'This one is *Har Gau*—that's steamed shrimp dumpling. Take some, Sister.' He passed the dish towards Jane.

Cautiously Jane manipulated her chopsticks and managed to get something on to her plate.

'It's very good,' she said, after the first mouthful. 'And what's in the other dishes?'

'This is *Fun Gwor*—steamed rice with pork, shrimp, and bamboo shoots, and this is *Pai Gwat*—spare ribs with red pepper sauce,' Nurse Wong indicated the different appetisers.

Jane soon found herself engrossed in the delights of the Chinese meal, and at the end of it she complimented Mary on her cooking. The maid smiled happily and retreated into the kitchen.

'I've enjoyed every meal I've had so far in Hong Kong,' Jane told the nurse. 'I didn't imagine the food would be so wonderful.'

'Just wait until Saturday night,' said Nurse Wong. 'I'm sure Dr Chandler will take you to a superb restaurant.'

'I expect he will,' said Jane, remembering that she must ring Martin to confirm their date, and also Matron for her room in the nurses' home. Or shall I be very wicked, she thought, and stay out all night in Hong Kong? Jane smiled to herself and then became aware that Chien Wong was watching her. Briskly, she jumped to her feet.

'Duty calls! We'd better get on with some work,' she said in an efficient voice. 'You're off duty aren't you, Nurse Wong?'

'Yes, Sister. I'm going over to Lantau island to meet some friends for the afternoon,' he said.

'Enjoy yourself,' said Jane, as she went off towards the patient's wing.

The intervening days passed uneventfully at the clinic and when Saturday evening arrived, Jane found herself looking forward to her night out with Martin. The boat sped across the water, carving trails of white foam in the calm surface of the bay. She leaned out and dabbled a hand idly in the cool water. Overhead, the last rays of the sun were dipping down to the horizon. There was an air of magic about the sunset here in Hong Kong.

The brilliant lights of Hong Kong Island beckoned her as the boat pulled in towards Victoria harbour. The sun had already disappeared behind the peak and the city was preparing for the pleasure and enjoyment of its night-life. When twilight falls, Hong Kong begins to light up with its own blend of oriental promise and western dining and dancing.

Jane stepped into a taxi and asked for the Mandarin Hotel. Martin had told her it was very near the waterfront but she preferred to arrive in style. Anyway, her expensive shoes were not made for walking on hard pavements—dancing, yes—but not walking! The taxi arrived at the Mandarin in a couple of minutes, and she took the lift up to the Captain's Bar, where she was to meet Martin. It turned out to be on the top floor of this very tall hotel and she caught a glimpse of the magnificent view of the harbour before she was shown to Martin's table. He was looking very handsome as he stood up to welcome her with a warm smile.

'You look fantastic!' was his reassuring greeting. 'What a fabulous dress!'

'Thank you,' Jane said, feeling self-assured and pleased that she had dared to wear her black, low-cut cocktail dress.

The waiter was hovering discreetly in the background, also casting admiring glances at this tall, attractive and sophisticated lady.

'We'll have a bottle of champagne,' said Martin to the waiter. Jane raised her eyebrows.

'To celebrate,' said Martin merrily.

'To celebrate what?' asked Jane, warming to his good humour.

'To celebrate the twilight, the beginning of a long night ahead of us—we don't need a *reason* to celebrate, do we?' he asked with a laugh.

The champagne arrived, jingling in its ice-bucket, the cork popped and the evening had really begun. After a couple of glasses of champagne Martin said they would have to go on to the next place.

'I've booked a table at the Furama, and it gets very busy on Saturday nights,' he explained.

Jane eyed the half-full bottle of champagne—but who was she to question his extravagance? He saw her quizzical look and laughed.

'The sky's the limit, tonight, my dear,' he said as he took her arm and steered her firmly towards the lift, tipping the waiter an exorbitant amount as they left.

Another taxi whisked them across to the Furama restaurant; a lift took them up to yet another fabulous view. And another waiter showed them to their table.

'It's moving!' said Jane in surprise, as they sat down.

Martin smiled across the table at her. 'The whole of this part of the restaurant revolves slowly so that you can see the entire view of Hong Kong during the course of your meal.'

Jane was mesmerised by the beauty of the lights shining in the harbour. She was aware that Martin was ordering more champagne and that the evening was beginning to take on a dream-like quality.

Suddenly she saw one of the waiters walking across the room towards her, carrying her handbag.

'You left this over there, madam,' he said politely, as he gave it to her.

'But I wasn't over there . . .' began Jane.

'Oh yes, you were,' laughed Martin. 'You must have put it down on the wall-ledge at the side of the table. It's only the floor that revolves—the walls stay still, of course!'

They both laughed, and Martin poured out some more champagne.

'Are you ready for dinner now?' he asked. 'I can recommend the buffet. It's absolutely out of this world.'

Jane glanced across at the superb display in the centre of the room and was impressed by what she saw.

'Lead me to it,' she said to Martin, enthusiastically.

She helped herself from a fabulous array of seafood and salads. There were also various attractive meat dishes, both European and Chinese, but it was quite impossible to sample everything.

The dessert course was also very spectacular and again Jane felt unable to do justice to the marvellous variety of dishes.

'This really has been a memorable evening, Martin,' she said as he paid the bill.

'*Has*?' he echoed. 'The night is young—it's only just beginning. We'll go on to the Hilton for some dancing. You're not tired, are you?' he asked.

'No, of course not,' she laughed gaily. 'I'm having a whale of a time.'

'Good,' he said, squeezing her arm gently. 'So am I.'

Their taxi drew up in front of the Hilton and they crossed the foyer to the inevitable lift. As the lift doors opened they saw that another couple were already in there, on their way up from the underground car park.

'Why, Mark! What a pleasant surprise,' said Martin, his arm still holding Jane as they stepped into the lift. 'And Nicola—what are you night-birds doing in this neck of the wood?'

'I could ask the same of you two,' said Mark

a trifle coolly. His petite, blonde companion stared across at Jane with a smug, complacent look.

'Good evening, Sister Marshall,' she said sweetly. 'I trust you're enjoying yourself here in Hong Kong.'

'Very much, thank you,' said Jane, trying to recover from the shock of seeing Mark and Nicola out together.

'And how do you find Cheung Lau? Personally, I would die of boredom stuck out there,' said Nicola, in a brittle voice.

'It's really very interesting,' Jane said coldly, carefully avoiding Mark's gaze. The effects of the champagne seemed to have suddenly worn off. The lift sped silently up to the top floor and the four of them got out.

'Have you booked a table?' Martin asked Mark.

'Yes,' Mark replied firmly. 'Our table's over there by the window.' He took hold of Nicola's arm and led her across the floor.

'Look's like he wants to be alone with his little bit of fluff,' smiled Martin. 'Come on Jane, this way.'

They were shown to a table at the other end of the room and Martin ordered some more champagne. Jane started to remonstrate on his extravagance but he silenced her with a wry grin.

'Silence woman! It's not every night I can

take you out. Just enjoy yourself. You worry too much—life's too short to waste it in worrying. Come and have a dance.'

They danced gently round the floor, passing within a few feet of the table where Mark and Nicola were deep in conversation.

How can he? thought Jane. I can accept that he's married, but not that's he's a philanderer. The music was soft and romantic, and the young singer was putting his heart and soul into the words. Jane pulled away from Martin's embrace and was relieved when the music changed to something more lively.

They took a break after a couple of dances and Jane sipped her drink, feeling some of the pleasure of the evening returning. It was impossible to feel sad for very long when Martin was around. He stood up suddenly, and she thought he was going to ask her to dance again.

'Do you mind if I go over and ask Nicola for a dance? Doesn't look like Mark's going to dance with her,' he smiled.

'Of course I don't mind,' Jane said. In fact, she felt quite relieved to be left alone for a while. Her back was towards the couple at the other side of the room and the lights were very dim, so she had no way of knowing what sort of reception they gave Martin—nor did she care.

The haunting melody of a song she had known a long time ago came over the microphone. Jane was suddenly aware that a tall figure was standing beside her.

'Mark!' she gasped, annoyed with herself for being taken unawares. He smiled down at her.

'Sorry if I startled you. May I sit down?'

'Why, of course,' Jane said, moving uneasily on her chair. 'Would you like some of this champagne?' she asked nervously and very quickly, to hide her confusion. 'I can call for another glass.' She started to raise her hand to attract a waiter, but he leaned across the table and put his hand over hers.

'Don't bother,' he said softly. 'I'll just have a sip of yours.' He picked up her glass and drank some, before setting it back down in front of her.

'I don't drink much, as you know.' He smiled at her across the table. 'I don't dance much, either, but I came to ask if you'd have this one with me, Jane.'

She hesitated, hardly daring to raise her eyes from the table. When she did so, she found that he was still watching her closely with those pools of devastating blue—those impossible eyes, which never failed to move her.

As if in a dream she stood up and walked towards the dance floor, knowing that he was just behind her. His arm slid around her waist and they started to dance. She put her hand lightly on his shoulder and the feeling of his body against hers reminded her of all those times they had been together long ago. Their bodies moved in unison across the dance floor. For someone who doesn't dance very much, you're remarkably expert tonight, thought Jane. But then, he was remarkably expert at most things. He was the most wonderful man she had ever loved. Yes, *loved*, she told herself—in the past tense.

The champagne had made her drowsy; she closed her eyes and moved round the floor in a trance, drifting imperceptibly back in time, with those wonderful arms holding her much too closely. She could feel every muscle of that hard, rippling body as the music swam over them.

With a start, Jane realised that the music had stopped, and yet they were still swaying together in the middle of the floor. She pulled herself reluctantly from his enthralling embrace and was aware that Nicola and Martin were standing near them.

'I've persuaded Nicola back to our table,' said Martin, in a matter of fact voice. 'We've got far too much champagne left. How about it, Mark?'

'No, I don't think so,' said Mark in a firm but distant voice. 'I've got to go now—but Nicola can stay, if she wants to.'

'No, I'll come with you, Mark,' said Nicola

softly, sidling up and putting her arm possessively through his. 'Goodnight everyone,' she added, giving a smug backward glance as the two of them walked away. Jane watched them disappear through the doorway, but Mark never turned round once.

If Martin had noticed the tension of those few parting seconds, he didn't remark on it but simply led Jane back to their table. He started to pour out more champagne, but Jane put her hand over her glass.

'I've had far too much already,' she smiled, with forced brightness. 'Do you think I could have a coffee?'

'Coffee?' he said, in mock horror. 'The lady wants *coffee*. What a funny idea! Actually, come to think of it, it's a brilliant idea. I'll lure you back to my bachelor pad and we'll sit on the balcony drinking coffee and watch the sunrise.'

'I'd much rather have a coffee now and then go back to the nurses' home for a few hours sleep,' she said. 'I do have to work tomorrow afternoon,' she added lamely.

'Work! What an ugly word,' he said, but he was already calling over a waiter to order the coffee.

'Next time, my girl, you won't get away so lightly.'

The coffee arrived and it was delicious. Jane smiled at Martin. 'Thanks for a marvellous evening,' she said. 'My first taste of Hong Kong night-life.'

'Ah, but it won't be your last, I can assure you,' he said as he called for the bill. 'This is only just the start. There are lots more places I can show you.'

He paid the bill and they were soon speeding along, up the hillside road in a taxi, to St Margaret's.

'Goodnight,' Jane said firmly at the door of the nurses' home.

'I thought you were going to ask me in for a night-cap?' Martin cajoled.

'I don't think Matron would approve,' smiled Jane.

'Come off it, Jane,' he said, in a bantering tone. 'You're a big girl now. This isn't the PTS at St Catherine's, you know.'

'No, it isn't,' she agreed, a far-away look in her eyes. 'Goodnight, Mark—I mean, Martin,' she corrected herself hastily.

He looked at her quizzically. 'Are you all right?' he asked, concerned.

'Yes, yes, I'm fine . . . Too much champagne,' she babbled. 'Goodnight, Martin, and thank you once again for a marvellous evening,' she added politely.

'Goodnight Jane,' he said, bending down to kiss her, but she had already retreated into the nurses' home.

She wanted to be alone in her room, away

from all the complications of the outside world. The room was exactly as she had left it, but someone had thoughtfully put a hospital night-gown on the bed—probably Matron, she thought. I must remember to leave a night-dress here for occasions like this.

Oh, my God, what a passion-killer! She picked up the long-sleeved cotton nightdress and eyed it critically. Still, it would keep her warm—the night air suddenly seemed very chilly. She walked across to close the windows and found herself gazing down at the ever-busy city, far below her.

'Goodnight, Hong Kong,' she whispered, as she closed the windows.

CHAPTER SIX

NEXT MORNING, as the boat sped across the water to Cheung Lau, Jane felt as if she were going home again. The familiar harbour with its multicoloured array of boats came into sight and she looked across to the foot of the hill, where the clinic was just discernible. A brisk walk through the Sunday morning crowds by the waterfront and she reached the relative peace of the clinic garden. The garden boy was watering his precious flowers, and he waved in a friendly way as he saw Jane walking up the front drive.

She went to her room and changed into her uniform before going to the patients' wing, where she found Nurse Lee and Nurse Wong. They greeted her warmly and assured her that all was well. It was good to be back.

Jane picked up her stethoscope and went in to see Carol, who was sitting up in bed reading. She smiled as Jane walked in.

'Hello, Sister. Have you come to check up on me?' she said mischievously. 'I haven't had a cigarette for days!'

'I should hope not,' said Jane with mock severity. 'Let's have a listen to your chest.'

Jane spent several minutes examining her, at the end of which she said, 'Well, there's a definite improvement. I think we'll be able to get you to theatre at St Margaret's this week.'

Carol's eyes showed her fear; she put out her hand and laid it on Jane's arm. 'Sister, will you be there?'

'No, Carol. I've got to stay here and look after the clinic,' she said in a firm but gentle voice. 'But I promise you that you'll be well looked after. The staff at St Margaret's are excellent.'

'Do I *have* to have this operation, Sister?' she asked in a pleading voice. 'I mean, don't you think this lump might just go away?'

'No, I don't,' said Jane calmly. 'And the sooner we check it out the better. So just be a brave girl, will you? I'm very proud of the way you've stopped smoking,' she added encouragingly. Carol smiled and settled back to reading her book as Jane went out.

The new baby was being fed by his ever-patient young mother when she arrived in the next room. He was making satisfied gurgling noises, so Jane left them to it, not wishing to disturb the feed.

She then went in to see Mr Kwan and noticed a marked improvement in his breathing and the colour of his skin. After examining him thoroughly, she told him in her halting

Cantonese that he would be able to go home in a few days.

'*Dor Jie*,' he said shyly—thank you.

After lunch there was very little nursing to be done, so Jane spent the afternoon familiarising herself with the equipment in the theatre and the treatment room. She wanted to ensure that she could deal with any emergency which might arise. She also wanted to be sure that she was fully prepared for the clinic in the morning. One of the doctors would be coming out to take it. Her heart beat a little faster. I hope it's not Dr Mark Frobisher, she lied to herself.

Monday morning found her, bright and early, in the treatment room, with everything prepared. From the window she could see a couple of patients already waiting outside, and then to her surprise she saw Dr Cynthia Martin walking up the drive. Jane put down the tray she was preparing and went to the front door to meet her.

'Welcome back, Cynthia,' she said with a smile. 'How are you?'

'Much better, thank you,' Cynthia said as she stepped into the reception area.

'Well, it's good to see you,' said Jane. 'We were quite worried about you.'

'Oh, I felt fine after a couple of days in bed. The last two days I've simply been idling around. It's nice to get out of the house. I

love coming over here,' she went on enthusiastically. 'What have you got for me this
morning?'

'I'd like you to take a look at the in-patients
first,' said Jane.

'OK, lead the way,' Cynthia said amicably.

The morning passed quite smoothly. There
were very few out-patients and those who
came required only minor treatment.

'They're breaking me in again gently,' said
Cynthia, as she packed her bag at the end
of the morning. 'They can see I've been off
sick.'

'Yes they're saving themselves for later in
the week,' said Jane, adding quite innocently,
'Who's coming over on Thursday?'

'No idea,' said Cynthia briskly. 'It's not me,
unfortunately—that I do know. I take the
ante-natal clinic at St Margaret's on Thurs-
days. Oh, I nearly forgot! We're having a few
friends over for lunch on Sunday. Are you
free?'

'I'm not sure,' the reply was quick and auto-
matic, almost brusque. Cynthia looked at her
quizzically and Jane, realising that her tone of
voice had been impolite, to say the least, tried
to soften its effect.

'I may have to work. It's terribly sweet of
you Cynthia. Can I let you know later in the
week?'

'Of course you can, but I would have

thought you could organise your own offduty hours,' she smiled.

'Oh, yes I do,' said Jane hastily. 'But I don't want to seem as if I'm putting on the others. I took the whole of Saturday night off . . .' As soon as she'd said it, she wished she hadn't.

'Oh, really? Go anywhere nice?' asked Cynthia.

'Yes. Martin took me round Hong Kong— showed me the night-life, lots of different places . . .' Jane babbled on breathlessly. Oh, please don't ask any more questions Cynthia, she prayed silently.

'Hong Kong's fantastic at night,' Cynthia was saying. 'I missed my Saturday night on the town this week—thought I ought to stay in and get myself fit for work again.'

Jane turned away and started tidying the treatment room to hide her confusion. She was dimly aware that Cynthia was still talking.

'Well, you'll let us know if you can make it on Sunday, Jane?'

'Yes, yes, of course. I'll ring you, Cynthia.' Then fully recovering her composure, she added, 'Can you stay for lunch now?'

'Sorry, I simply haven't time. Got a hectic schedule today,' said Cynthia as she made for the front door. 'Pity, really, I hear you've got a marvellous cook.' She stepped out into the sunlight. 'Next time, perhaps. Goodbye,

Jane,' and she was off down the drive.

Jane turned back into the clinic and breathed a sigh of relief. She most definitely would not accept Cynthia's invitation to lunch. It would be unbearable to see them together—and the children too. She walked hurriedly along to her room to freshen up before lunch. Closing the door, she sat down on the narrow bed and stared out of the window for several minutes. Gradually her thoughts cleared.

I can't go on running away, she told herself. I've got to face up to the present. Perhaps it would be a good idea to see the family situation, so that I can convince myself that it's over, once and for all.

Martin came to take the clinic on Thursday and took Carol back to St Margaret's by helicopter for her operation, which was scheduled for Friday. Jane had found herself fully occupied during the week and realised, as she said goodbye to her patient, that she still hadn't phoned Cynthia.

She put a call through to the house and was relieved that it was Cynthia's amah who answered. Yes, she would pass the message on that Sister Marshall was coming to lunch on Sunday.

'Thank you for calling, Sister,' she said politely, in perfect English. The dye was cast—there was no escape now.

Whether it was the worry about Carol's breast operation at St Margaret's or her own doubting fears over the forthcoming Sunday lunch, Jane found herself decidedly ill-humoured on Friday. She woke up with a splitting headache, and found herself half hoping that she was going down with Cynthia's flu. That would certainly excuse her from facing up to her ordeal on Sunday. Somehow she managed to get through the morning; hard work was always her panacea whenever she felt under the weather. She waited until late-afternoon before phoning St Margaret's to ask about Carol.

'Sister Marshall, we were just going to ring you,' came the reassuring voice of the theatre sister. 'Good news, we've done a biopsy and the tumour is benign.'

'Oh, that's excellent,' said Jane with relief. 'Have you told her yet?'

'No, she's still a bit drowsy after the anaesthetic. Dr Frobisher's going to explain everything to her when she's fully recovered,' theatre sister's voice continued. 'I wonder if she could come back to you for a few days post-operative care next week, Sister Marshall? She especially asked to be transferred back to Cheung Lau before we took her into theatre.'

'By all means, Sister. Whenever you like. We'll keep a bed for her,' said Jane.

'Thank you, Sister. Would Monday be convenient?'

'Of course,' said Jane.

The good news about the biopsy was soon passed on to Nurse Lee and Nurse Wong, who were delighted.

'So, no admissions on Sunday while I'm away,' said Jane with a smile. 'That is, unless you really have to. I suppose we ought to think about sending our young mum back to her family. That would clear one bed.'

'And Mr Kwan is much better, Sister,' said Nurse Wong.

'Yes, we'll see what Dr Frobisher thinks on Monday,' said Jane, adding hastily, 'I think it's his turn to take the clinic.'

Jane sent both her nurses off duty on Saturday and spent a quiet day by herself with the in-patients. There was no trace of her headache of the previous day, so she knew that she was going to be perfectly fit for the lunch party on Sunday.

When she actually found herself speeding across the water towards Hong Kong the next day, she had a feeling of exhilaration. It was almost as if she had surmounted an incredibly high obstacle. At least, she was on her way to doing just that, she thought wryly.

It was a superb day—blue sky, blue sea, lightly flecked waves, glorious sunshine.

Nothing can spoil it, she told herself, as she breathed in the tangy salt freshness of the sea air.

Victoria harbour came into view and she was soon in a taxi, driving up towards the peak. The address Cynthia had given her was about half a mile from the hospital, but on the other side of the peak. The taxi rounded a bend and there it was—a most beautiful house set back from the road in a setting of mature trees and shrubs. The taxi ground to a halt on the gravel drive. Jane paid the driver and went towards the front door, her heart beating wildly. A white-coated servant opened the door and took her along a corridor to the other side of the house. Through the open windows she could see crowds of people round a lovely pool, drinking, laughing, talking loudly; there were two adorable little children splashing around in the shallow end.

So this is their domestic bliss, thought Jane wretchedly, wishing she could turn round and run away from the idyllic scene. This could all have been mine—if only I hadn't insisted on my career. She could see Mark in the midst of a crowd of admiring friends. He looked across towards her, but she averted her eyes quickly, hoping that someone would rescue her. At that moment Cynthia saw her and pushed her way through.

'Jane, dear, how lovely to see you,' she said,

taking her by the arm. 'Come and meet my husband.'

'But I . . .'

'Darling, this is the newest member of the Cheung Lau team.'

Jane looked at the smiling face of the stranger in front of her. Dimly she was aware that Cynthia was saying, 'Jane, this is my husband, Dave Weston.'

'Well, hello there,' she heard Dave say from somewhere in the distance. 'Nice to have you around.'

'Dave's only just got back from the States this morning,' said Cynthia. 'He's been away at a boring medical conference all the time I was ill—what a time to choose!' she laughed.

'Well, I'm home now, darling,' he smiled at her lovingly. 'Always glad to be back. Let me get you a drink Jane. You look as if you could use one.'

'Yes, are you all right?' asked Cynthia in a concerned voice. 'You look as if you've seen a ghost!'

'I'm fine . . . I've been a bit under the weather,' Jane stammered. 'Headache and so on.'

'Oh, dear! Hope it's not my flu,' exclaimed Cynthia. 'Get her a drink darling—kill a few germs, anyway,' she added laughingly.

'Champagne OK?' asked Dave.

'Fine.' The strength was coming back into

her legs. For one awful moment she had thought she was going to faint. She looked across at Mark, but he was now deeply engrossed in conversation with the tiny blonde figure of Nicola.

What a fool I've been, thought Jane. I never doubted the fact that he and Cynthia were married. Dave Weston handed her a glass of champagne.

'There you go,' he said, smiling amicably. 'Cheers, Jane.'

'Cheers!' She took a large gulp of her sparkling drink, smiled at her host and started to feel much better. The situation had changed altogether now. She began to feel light-headed! She simply had to see Mark and explain.

'Did you bring a swim-suit?' Cynthia was asking her.

'No, I didn't know you had a pool.'

'I should have told you,' Cynthia raised an eyebrow. 'We always have a swim before lunch. Doesn't matter—I can lend you one of mine.' Some of the guests had already retired to the changing-rooms to prepare for the ritual swim.

'Come up to my room,' Cynthia suggested. 'We'll see what we can find.' She led the way through the house and up a sumptuous staircase to the master bedroom. It was an enormous room, delightfully furnished in oriental style, and it overlooked the swimming-pool.

'This is a lovely room, Cynthia,' said Jane admiringly. 'And such a beautiful house.'

'Yes, isn't it,' said Cynthia as she rooted through one of her drawers. 'We're very lucky, Dave and I. Here, how about this one? I think that might fit you; it's a bikini I bought a couple of years ago, in a hopeful mood. I've never been slim enough to wear it but it should look good on you.'

Jane took the miniscule white bikini from Cynthia and smiled. 'Thank you.' Sitting down on one of the bamboo chairs by the window, she suddenly felt that she had to confide in her hostess.

'Do you know, Cynthia—I honestly thought you were married to Mark.'

Cynthia burst out laughing. 'Oh, you didn't! How priceless! I expect you'd heard of our engagement when we first left St Catherine's?'

'Yes, it was the talk of the hospital at the time,' said Jane, relieved that she could speak about it at last.

'I bet it was,' said Cynthia, adding, 'I mean it was all so sudden and out of the blue—so unexpected.'

Jane nodded and held her breath, waiting to hear the full story.

'No, it was just a few weeks of mutual attraction—we were never in love,' said Cynthia. 'We were both lonely, away from home and, now I come to think of it, Mark was definitely on the rebound.' Cynthia smiled at Jane, light suddenly dawning. 'Yes,' she said to Jane, softly, 'Mark was trying to recover from some unrequited romance, but he never succeeded. Our engagement soon turned into a sort of friendly brother and sister relationship and we both decided to break it off. Soon after that I met Dave, and hey presto!'

'You and Dave seem very well suited,' Jane said.

'I suppose you could say we got married and lived happily ever after,' laughed Cynthia. 'Not *strictly* true—we have our disagreements, but nothing serious. If you can combine marriage with your career, I can thoroughly recommend it.' Then, lowering her voice, she added, 'But you'd better do something about it, before that little minx gets her claws into him.'

From the window they could see Mark swimming strongly across the pool, a tiny blonde figure in hot pursuit.

'Put that bikini on and get yourself down there quickly,' said Cynthia with a conspiratorial smile. They looked at each other and laughed.

'I'll be as quick as a flash,' said Jane, already unbuttoning her dress.

'See that you are—there's not a minute to

lose,' giggled Cynthia as she went out, closing the door behind her.

Jane glanced at herself in the mirror. The attractive tan, which she had managed to acquire during off-duty hours on Cheung Lau, looked very becoming in the white bikini. She put a comb through her dark hair and then stepped back from the mirror. In actual fact, when stripped of her sophisticated dress, she looked very little different from the young girl of eight years ago.

She ran lightly down the stairs and out to the edge of the pool, aware of the admiring glances as she plunged into the water. As she surfaced, someone placed a hand on her shoulder. Eagerly she turned, but found it was Martin.

'My, that was a spectacular dive,' he said. 'Didn't know we had a mermaid in our midst!'

'Thank you.' Jane smiled, looking around her in the pool as they swam along together. 'What a lovely party,' she called over the noise of the splashing water and the merry voices.

'Yes, isn't it,' said Martin. 'Good fun, Cynthia and Dave. I always enjoy coming here.' After a couple of lengths he suggested a breather.

'How about another drink Jane,' he gasped. 'I can't keep up with you.'

Jane climbed out and Martin led her across to a table by the poolside. With a start, she realised that Mark and Nicola were already sitting there.

'We seem to bump into all the same people in our off duty hours,' said Martin amicably as they sat down at the table.

'How are things over on Cheung Lau?' asked Mark politely.

'Fine.' Jane looked into the piercing blue eyes, wishing that everyone else would disappear so that they could be alone together. 'I was relieved with the result of the biopsy,' she added in her most professional voice.

'Yes, so was I,' said Mark. 'She's a very lucky young woman. I'll bring her back tomorrow when I come to take the clinic.'

'Look, we're not here to talk shop,' put in Martin quickly. 'Have some more champagne you two, and spare us the medical details.' He poured more. 'Nicola—more champagne?'

'Yes please,' the little blonde held out her glass. She had been watching Jane and Mark very carefully.

'I'd love to see your little clinic,' she said in a quiet voice. 'Mark, do you think you could arrange to take me with you one day?'

'Why, of course,' he turned and smiled at her. 'Actually I shall need an escort nurse with the patient tomorrow, so we'll see what we can do.'

'Oh, that would be great,' she said, flashing him a brilliant smile. Then, turning to Jane, she asked, 'Don't you find it's a bit lonely out there—I mean, cut off from civilisation?'

'Not at all. It's a delightful little place and not too far from Hong Kong,' said Jane in a cool voice.

'Did you come over this morning?' Nicola continued in the same sweet-little-girl voice.

'Yes, it was lovely out there on the water,' Jane replied smoothly.

'Be even better tonight, in the sunset,' said Martin. 'Why don't I take you back to your little island after the party. How about it Jane?'

'Well, I don't know. I'm not sure what's happening,' she faltered, aware that Mark's eyes were upon her.

'What could possibly happen to prevent you watching our spectacular sunset?' said Martin in a persuasive voice.

'I, er, I think I may go back before sunset,' Jane murmured hesitantly. 'There's a lot to do at the clinic.'

'Nonsense!' laughed Martin. 'You've got a brilliant staff out there on Cheung Lau—hand-picked, weren't they Mark?'

Mark nodded and said in a neutral voice, 'I'm sure you can stay as long as you please, Jane.' The blue eyes looking into hers were those of a stranger. She turned away hastily.

'There you are, then,' Martin was saying happily. 'If the boss thinks it's OK you can stop worrying. Enjoy yourself, girl.'

Jane smiled at Martin. He was trying so hard, and he was a likeable sort of man. If only . . . she stood up decisively and made for the pool.

'Let's have another swim—race you to the other end,' she called over her shoulder.

'Hey—wait for me,' shouted Martin as he put his drink down on the table and pursued the bikini-clad figure into the water.

Jane struck out swiftly and touched the bar at the other end of the pool before Martin came splashing up behind her.

'That was cheating,' he said laughingly. 'You had a head start. This time we'll both set off together. On your marks, get set—go!'

They raced back down the pool. Several of the guests gathered at the edge to watch the impromptu race and cheered as the two swimmers touched the bar simultaneously.

'Dead heat,' called Cynthia, coming up to the end of the pool. 'Such energy in the middle of the day! Well done, you two!'

Dave was close behind his wife and smiled approvingly as Martin and Jane climbed out, laughing and shaking the water off.

'You must be hungry after all that exertion,' he said. 'I've lit the barbecue on the terrace over there. Come and have some food.' Then, raising his voice he called, 'Lunch everybody—come and get it!'

The guests drifted across to the terrace where there was a delicious smell of charcoal-grilled steaks. Dave was very much in command of the grilling part of the operation. Cynthia and her amah had prepared huge bowls of delicious salads which were set out on a long table for the guests to help themselves from.

As Jane crossed over to the salad table Cynthia whispered with a smile, 'You're still with the wrong man.'

Jane shrugged. 'I know, but what . . .' Martin had joined her so she quickly turned it into, 'What delicious food Cynthia—marvellous party!'

'I'm so glad you're enjoying yourself,' Cynthia said with a whimsical grin, and moved on to help the next guest.

Martin and Jane went back to the poolside table to eat their lunch. Out of the corner of her eye Jane could see Nicola manoeuvring Mark over to another table. Martin noticed it too. He turned to Jane and said brightly, 'Now I've got you all to myself.'

Jane smiled. 'Aren't you the lucky one? My steak is delicious,' she added. 'How's yours?'

'Tastes all the better for being in such attractive company,' he said, grinning happily at her. 'I was quite serious about taking you back across the water tonight, you know. I've got my own boat—I'd love to show it to you.'

'OK why not?' Jane said frivolously. 'But what about Jim, the boatman? He'll be waiting for me.'

'No problem—I'll ring him after lunch. He'll be relieved to take a half day off,' said Martin.

'You're very persuasive,' Jane said.

'I know,' he grinned. 'I like to get my own way.'

'Yes, I can see that,' she parried.

The afternoon sun was very hot and some of the guests retired to the shade of the trees, but the sun-worshippers remained by the pool. Jane and Martin stretched out at the edge of the water on loungers. A lethargic drowsiness was creeping over Jane and she closed her eyes and drifted imperceptibly into sleep.

Some time later she was aware that a tall figure was standing in front of her, talking quietly to Martin.

'I hope you enjoy your sunset sail,' the familiar voice was saying. Then, as he noticed her stirring, Mark added, 'Sorry Jane, I didn't mean to wake you.' He was looking down admiringly at the slim, attractive figure of the girl who had once meant so much to him.

Jane sat up, startled at the unexpected awakening.

'I've got to go now,' Mark was saying. 'Enjoy the trip back to Cheung Lau. It should be very beautiful out there this evening.'

Did Jane detect a tone of wistfulness in his voice, or was it just her imagination? Their eyes met and this time she didn't turn away, but allowed herself to melt into them—but only for a second, for she heard Mark continue in his professional voice.

'Will you prepare a room for our post-operative patient tomorrow, Jane?'

'Yes, of course,' she said, smoothly in control of the situation. 'Goodbye, Mark.'

'Goodbye.' The tall figure strode over to the terrace where Jane could see a petite blonde waiting impatiently. She turned back to Martin.

'Do you think it's too soon after lunch for a swim?' she asked breezily.

'Too soon?' he echoed. 'You've been asleep for ages, my girl. I've been rushing around making phone calls and getting everything organised, while you lazed around here.'

'Really?' Jane smiled as she jumped off the sun-bed. 'It's time for another dip then. I need waking up!'

They dived into the pool and swam steadily together for a few minutes. As they climbed out they noticed that tea was being served on the terrace.

'I think I'll go and change,' Jane said. 'Be back soon.' She made her way up the staircase and across the landing towards Cynthia's room. As she did so, the door to Dave's study opened and he and Mark came out, deeply engrossed in conversation.

'I have to go over to Cheung Lau tomorrow,' Mark was saying. 'So if you could take a look at the post-operative cases . . .' He stopped dead in his tracks as he came face to face with Jane.

'Mark! I thought you'd gone,' she said quietly.

'We've been having a useful medical conference—filling me in on the details,' smiled Dave. 'Sorry to keep you, Mark.'

'Not at all,' he said. As Dave made for the stairs, Jane found herself alone at last with Mark. She felt suddenly very unsure of herself.

'That's a very attractive bikini you're wearing,' he said, with that heart-melting smile that Jane found so irresistible.

'Thank you. I borrowed it from Cynthia. I was just on my way to change out of it,' she faltered.

'Were you now,' he said smoothly as he moved towards her. He put out his hand and touched the ribbon bow on one of her shoulders. 'Would you like me to help you?' he asked softly, pulling gently on the ribbon. A petulant voice from the staircase interrupted them.

'Mark, how much longer will you be? You said you were going to give me a lift.'

Jane turned and fled into Cynthia's bedroom. She couldn't bear to see the two of them together again today. Quickly she changed into her cream linen dress and went down for tea. Anyone watching the tall slim figure moving easily amongst the guests would not have guessed at the turmoil inside her.

As twilight began to fall Martin and Jane took their leave of Cynthia and Dave and drove off down the hillside towards Hong Kong. Lights were beginning to twinkle everywhere. As they reached the harbour there was a multicoloured iridescence on the water. Jane stepped onto Martin's boat as if in a dream and allowed herself to soak up the magic of the sunset as the boat sped across the water. The bright orange sun was sinking slowly beneath the horizon, casting long, straight lines which pierced into the dark blue depths of the water. It was too beautiful for words; neither of them spoke until they were almost at Cheung Lau and then Martin broke the silence.

'I told you it was a marvellous sight,' he said softly.

Jane nodded. She didn't trust herself to speak at that moment. Suddenly she was aware that he had put his arm around her shoulders. She shivered involuntarily.

'Jane, you're cold,' he said, in a concerned voice. 'Let me get you a sweater.'

'No, I'm all right Martin,' she said, sitting stiffly upright in the circle of his arm. 'Anyway, we're nearly there.'

'Yes. I hope you're going to offer me a nightcap this time.' Jane sighed wearily.

'I've got some coffee,' she said politely.

'Fine.' They were entering the harbour. The lights from the moored boats lit up the darkness as Martin tied up the boat and helped Jane ashore.

They walked in silence along the path to the clinic and as they approached they saw that there was a light in the reception area. Nurse Wong was sitting at the desk writing. He smiled and stood up as Jane and Martin arrived.

'Everything OK?' asked Jane.

'Yes, no problems, Sister. Did you enjoy your party?' he asked.

'It was great fun.' Jane forced a smile. 'We've come back for some coffee before Dr Chandler heads for the mainland.'

'Mary will make some for you. I'll just go and tell her. Why don't you go and sit on the veranda?' Nurse Wong suggested.

Martin looked crestfallen as the figure of the male nurse disappeared towards the kitchen in search of coffee.

'I thought we were going to have coffee in your room,' he said quietly, as he followed Jane out on to the veranda.

'Did you?' asked Jane brightly. 'No, it's much more pleasant out here. Mm . . . can you smell those flowers, Martin?'

'Look, Jane,' he began, in a tone more serious than he had ever used before.

'I didn't come all this way to discuss flowers. You know very well . . .' He broke off as Mary came out with the coffee, closely followed by Nurse Wong.

'Ah how splendid—you've brought three cups, Nurse Wong,' said Jane. 'I'm so glad you're going to join us. Dr Chandler and I were just discussing the flowers, and I know so very little about the garden here. Nurse Wong is an expert,' she added, trying to keep the relief from her voice.

'Really,' Martin said drily. 'How fascinating.' He sipped his coffee for a few seconds in silence, then some of his natural good humour returned. 'I'll have to ask you to show me round the garden one day, Nurse Wong.'

'That would be a pleasure, Doctor,' said Nurse Wong.

Martin drank his coffee and stood up. 'Well, I'll leave you two to the delights of your unspoilt island and get back to civilisation,' he said.

Nurse Wong stood up, too. 'Goodnight, Dr Chandler,' he said as he went through into the clinic.

Jane smiled. 'Thanks, Martin. It's been a lovely day—and thank you for bringing me back.'

'Well, at least I got a coffee—better than last time,' he said wryly. 'Goodnight Jane.' He leaned down and kissed her gently on the cheek. He turned to wave as he reached the gates of the clinic, but Jane had already gone inside.

Alone in her room, she was thinking about the events of that long day. If only she had known what she knew now. If only she hadn't jumped to conclusions so easily. If only . . .

She lay down on her bed and closed her eyes, remembering the gentle feeling of Mark's fingers on her shoulder. She lightly traced her fingers over the place where he had touched her. Shivers ran down her spine.

Tomorrow, she thought. Yes, tomorrow he'll be here, and somehow I must talk to him alone . . .

CHAPTER SEVEN

JANE started Monday morning with a frenzy of activity, for she wanted to be quite sure that everything was prepared before Mark arrived. As she heard the whirring of the helicopter overhead her heart started to beat faster, but she willed herself to adopt her professional manner. Outwardly she looked very calm, but inwardly she was trembling with anticipation.

The helicopter touched down at the side of the clinic and Jane said quietly, 'Nurse Wong, would you go and meet Dr Frobisher? He may need some help with the post-operative patient.'

'Of course, Sister,' the male nurse said, setting off along the path in the bright sunlight.

Jane watched as the helicopter doors opened and Mark climbed out, followed by Nurse Nicola Bryant with Carol, who looked quite strong and certainly much happier than when she had left the clinic before her operation. She waved to Jane when she saw her standing in the doorway.

'Hello, Sister,' she called. 'I've come to pester you again!'

'It's nice to have you back, Carol,' said Jane

115

with a smile, adding, 'your room's all ready for you. Nurse Lee, would you take Carol and settle her in? I'll be along in a minute.'

Jane had deliberately avoided looking at Mark and Nicola. Now she turned to them and said, 'Nicola, perhaps you'd like to go and help Nurse Lee with Carol?'

Nicola paused for a moment before she replied, very sweetly, 'I think Dr Frobisher wants me to help him here with the out-patients.'

Jane drew in a deep breath and said firmly, 'I think we shall all be involved with the out-patients, Nurse, but at this particular moment . . .'

'At this particular moment, I should like to do a round of the in-patients,' interrupted Mark decisively, adding in a cool professional voice, 'so if you'd like to lead the way, Sister . . .'

Jane was mortified. How dare he speak to her like that in front of one of the nurses? Out of the corner of her eye, she could see a smug little smile on Nicola's face.

'This way, Dr Frobisher,' she grated, swallowing her pride, as she strode purposefully along the corridor to the in-patients' wing. She was aware that Mark's tall figure was right behind her, while the tiny blonde pattered beside him, trying to keep up the brisk pace.

'What a sweet little clinic,' said Nicola

breathlessly. 'Oh, can I have a look in the operating-theatre?' They were just passing the door, but Jane walked quickly past it.

'Later, Nurse Bryant. We've got work to do first,' she muttered.

They arrived at Mr Kwan's room and went in. He was sitting up in bed, surrounded by his family. Jane had not seen them arrive—they must have simply wandered in through the windows. As soon as they saw the doctor, they started to fire questions at him in rapid Cantonese. The elder son was chief spokesman and Jane gathered that they were wanting to take their father home, but she was glad that Mark was there to act as interpreter.

He was nodding his head and replying fluently to the questions. When he turned to look at Jane, it was to ask, 'Has there been any recurrence of the cyanosis, Sister?'

'No, Doctor,' Jane replied.

'And his respiration? Has he required oxygen recently?'

'No, Doctor.' Jane crossed to the bed and prepared Mr Kwan for a cardiac examination. Mark listened intently with his stethoscope while the relatives waited quietly on the veranda.

When he had finished Mark stood back from the bed and smiled reassuringly at Mr Kwan. Then, turning to Jane, he said, 'He can be discharged today, Sister. Perhaps you'd like to tell the relatives that he will still require plenty of rest at home.'

Jane took several seconds to make a mental translation of the necessary phrases. Mark saw her hesitation and broke in irritably. 'Oh, don't worry, Sister. I'll tell them myself.' He walked out to the veranda and spent a few minutes speaking to the relatives.

'Nurse Bryant, would you help this patient pack his belongings and prepare him for discharge,' he requested on his return. And to Jane, 'I've asked the relatives to bring him back to the clinic on Thursday for another check-up. Now, will you show me the next patient, please.'

He gave a few words of advice to Mr Kwan and then followed Jane into the next room. Jane was half expecting a remonstration from Nicola, who was being left behind, so she moved on quickly.

The young mother and baby made a pretty sight, sitting in a chair by the window. Mark examined the baby first and then the mother, after which he declared they were both fit and well and could go home. Jane looked slightly dubious.

'I'm not too sure about the home situation,' she said quietly.

Mark turned to speak to the patient. After a few brief questions he seemed satisfied and said to Jane, 'There's no medical reason why she shouldn't go. Her family are anxious to have her back. We can't keep her here permanently, just for a rest cure, you know.'

'I suppose you're right,' she said. Then, remembering their professional relationship, she added, 'Thank you Doctor. I'll arrange for her to be discharged as soon as possible.'

They went in to see Carol, who was sitting in a chair and looking out at the garden. 'I like being here,' she said to Jane. 'It's so peaceful. How long can I stay?'

Mark smiled. 'You can stay just as long as it takes for the breast wound to heal and then we shall turn you out—oh, and *no* cigarettes young lady,' he added.

'As if I would,' said Carol, grinning mischieviously.

'There's no need to touch the dressing today, Sister,' said Mark. 'Have a look at it tomorrow. Goodbye, Carol. Behave yourself.'

Mark waited for Jane to show him out of the room, but instead she walked out on to the veranda, saying casually, 'We'll go back to the treatment room this way, Doctor. It's much more pleasant.'

Mark followed her outside and along the veranda towards the front of the clinic. Jane suddenly stopped and leaned against the wooden rail. Mark came alongside her and paused in front of her, looking quizzically into her eyes. He noticed the distress and tension, and his cool, distant manner changed immediately. Taking hold of her hand, he asked, very gently, 'What is it, Jane?'

'Mark, I've got to talk to you,' she said quickly and breathlessly. 'I've made such a silly mistake.'

'A mistake? Here at the clinic?' he interrupted anxiously.

'No, no. Not a medical mistake,' she said hastily, hearing his sigh of relief even as she spoke. 'No, I've been so stupid—Mark I honestly thought . . .'

'Ah, there you are!' Nicola's brittle voice cut in, as she came tripping along the veranda. 'I've looked everywhere for you. Mr Kwan and his relatives are waiting in reception for the medication Dr Frobisher prescribed.'

Her eyes flickered for an instant at the two of them together before she glanced away and looked across the garden. 'What a beautiful garden you have here,' she said, smiling sweetly at Jane. 'I suppose you sit out there cultivating your tan?'

'When I have time,' said Jane icily as she turned and headed for the reception area. She could hear Nicola prattling to Mark as they followed her, but he did not appear to be listening. At any rate, he didn't make any reply to her chatter.

'Nurse Bryant, I think you can help Nurse

Wong in the treatment room,' he said, as they reached the reception area. 'Sister and I can cope with the out-patients here.'

Nicola looked as if she were about to object, but Mark added firmly, 'Thank you, Nurse Bryant. That will be all for the moment.'

Nicola pouted her lip, but went off sulkily into the treatment room. Mark turned to Jane and said, 'It's sometimes very difficult to keep these young nurses in check.'

'Well, if you will encourage them in your off-duty hours . . .' began Jane. Almost as she said it, she wanted to bite her tongue off. Oh heavens, that's torn it, she thought, seeing the black look he gave her as he settled himself behind the main desk.

'Bring in the first patient, Sister,' he said coolly.

Jane turned away and went out to the waiting area.

'Will you come this way, please?' she said absently to a young woman sitting under the trees. Seeing the look of consternation on the patient's face she repeated her question in Cantonese, smiling reassuringly. The young woman waddled inside and Jane went along to the treatment room to make preparations for an ante-natal examination.

The morning continued uneventfully and Mark seemed pleased with the smooth-running atmosphere of the clinic. He was taking a short coffee-break with Jane and Nurse Lee, when he suddenly said, 'Congratulations Sister. You seem to have everything under control here.'

'Thank you,' Jane said quietly. She hoped that Nurse Lee was going to leave them together, but she just sat there, drinking coffee, oblivious to the fact that she was in the way.

It was Mark who stood up first. Speaking in his professional voice he said, 'Shall we go back to the patients, Sister?'

Nurse Lee jumped hurriedly to her feet, and followed Mark and Jane along to the reception area. Nurse Wong was waiting for them.

'I've got a patient in the treatment room and I'd like you to see him, Doctor,' he said.

'Yes, of course,' Mark replied, as the male nurse led the way.

A man of between sixty and seventy was lying on one of the couches, looking very distressed. Jane could hear that he had respiratory problems, so she wound up the head of the couch and placed a pillow behind his head. He gave a harsh, tearing cough and put a hand over his chest, where he was obviously experiencing pain. Mark gave him a thorough examination before asking him a number of questions in Cantonese. Turning to Jane, he said quietly, 'I think we'll have to keep him in.'

'I want to go home,' said the old man, with difficulty.

Mark turned in surprise. 'I'm sorry,' he said to the patient. 'I didn't realise you spoke English.'

'I want to go home,' repeated the man firmly, and a little louder this time.

'I'm afraid that's out of the question,' Mark said. 'We shall have to keep you here for a few days. Sister will look after you.'

'Do you have any relatives with you?' Jane asked kindly.

'Sister, I've already established that he lives by himself,' put in Mark irritably. 'That's one of the reasons we have to admit him. I do wish you'd listen when I'm talking to the patients.'

'I'm doing the best I can, Doctor,' said Jane coldly. 'My Cantonese is obviously not up to your standard. Perhaps when I've lived out here a little longer . . .'

'Yes, yes, I realise the problems,' Mark said hurriedly. 'Now, let's admit the patient. Nurse Wong, will you see to it please? At least you speak the language.'

He turned and started to go back into the reception area, calling over his shoulder, 'Shall we see the other patients now, Sister?'

Jane followed quietly behind him, aware that Nurse Bryant's pretty blue eyes were twinkling merrily as she helped Nurse Wong to transfer the patient on to a trolley.

Mark sat down at his desk and started scribbling out a treatment sheet for the new patient.

'He's obviously neglected himself, to get into this state,' Mark said, looking up from his desk. 'He must have had repeated attacks of acute bronchitis, which is why it's now chronic. We can ease the condition with antibiotics and general nursing care, but there isn't much we can do when he goes home again.'

Jane picked up the treatment sheet and her eyes scanned over it quickly. 'I'll go and organise this at once,' she said in her brisk, professional manner.

'Thank you, Sister,' Mark said in the same detached tone. 'Nurse Lee, would you bring in the next patient, please.'

At the end of the out-patient clinic, when all the patients had been seen, Jane went back into the reception area. Mark was writing up some notes at the desk, while Nicola was thumbing idly through a pile of magazines.

'Everything finished, I see,' Jane said in a cool voice. 'Have you enjoyed your morning with us, Nurse Bryant?'

'Oh, yes I have.' The young nurse smiled sweetly. 'It's been such a change from St Margaret's. Everything's so quaint, so, er, primitive! I wouldn't like to be here all the time, though. I'd miss Hong Kong—I mean, there's nothing to do here in your off duty time, is there?'

Jane swallowed hard. 'I don't easily get bored myself,' she said. 'There's always something to do.'

'Oh, I'm sure there is,' Nicola said in the same sweet voice. Then, still smiling, she said, 'Are you coming to the party on Sunday?'

'Which party?' Jane asked without much interest.

'Mark's parents are having a lunch party at their beach house. I thought everyone . . .' Her voice trailed off as she realised that Mark was looking across from his desk.

'Thank you, Nurse Bryant,' he said icily. 'I can arrange my own social life.'

Jane felt acutely embarrassed. She turned away and started towards the treatment room, saying as she went, 'If you don't mind, I've got work to do . . .'

'Jane!' Mark's voice was firm and imperious. She turned automatically to face him. 'I was meaning to invite you, but we've been so busy this morning, and I hate mixing my professional and social life.' He paused, as if to emphasise his point, then continued quietly. 'I hope you're free on Sunday. My parents are hoping that everyone will come.'

She avoided his eyes and took her time before replying, in a cool voice, 'I wouldn't want to disappoint your parents. I'll see what I can do about arranging some time off. Now you must excuse me.'

She went into the treatment room, straight
out on to the veranda and along to her room.
She wasn't going to give Nicola the satisfaction
of seeing how upset she was. The noise of the
helicopter told Jane that they had gone, and
she felt nothing but a sense of relief.

For the next few days she was too busy to
think about anything except the smooth-
running of the clinic. Word had got around
among the boat people and more and more
patients were turning up, not only in the morn-
ings, but at all hours of the day. Jane didn't
want to discourage them, so she insisted that
everyone was seen, no matter how minor the
ailment.

When Martin arrived to do the clinic on
Thursday he was amazed to read through the
treatment report. 'Looks like we're going to
have to expand soon, Jane,' he said.

'I agree absolutely,' she said. 'I broached
the subject once with Mark. He wasn't very
forthcoming at the time, but it was in the early
days, before we got really busy.'

'Well, I'll mention it to him when I get back
to St Margaret's,' said Martin. 'You're going
to need an extension of the existing building. That's no problem—there are plenty of
builders and carpenters on the island. But it'll
take time to get the plans drawn up and official
approval. I'm sure we could arrange to give
you another nurse at once though. How about

Nurse Bryant? She's been out here, hasn't she?'

'No thanks.' Jane's reply was instantaneous and very sharp.

Martin looked at her quizzically. 'You don't like her, do you?' he said.

'Not much,' replied Jane briefly. 'No, I'm quite happy with my existing staff. Nurse Lee and Nurse Wong are excellent. I think we can cope, for the moment. Now, shall I bring in the first patient, Doctor?'

'Thank you, Sister.' He smiled broadly and settled back in his chair, drumming with a pencil on his desk.

At the end of the morning session Martin stayed for lunch. He was most appreciative of Mary's cooking and made flattering remarks as she served them with fish in ginger, steamed prawns, rice and vegetables.

'You're wasted out here, Mary,' he said. 'You ought to have your own restaurant in Hong Kong. You'd make a bomb.'

Mary smiled shyly and went back into the kitchen.

'For heaven's sake, don't put ideas into her head,' laughed Jane. 'Mary's cooking is one of the compensations for living miles away from civilisation.'

'You're not *miles* away,' said Martin. 'It takes only a few minutes by helicopter, and not very long by boat—which reminds me, when are you going to come out in my boat again? We could make a whole day of it. Take a picnic lunch and land on a desert island somewhere.'

Jane smiled. 'I don't think I can take a whole day off at the moment.'

'There you go again! Work always comes first with you,' Martin said in a bantering tone. Then, slightly more seriously, he added, 'I bet you're going to take Sunday off to go out to Sheko.'

'Sheko?' Jane looked puzzled. 'Where's Sheko?'

'That's where the Frobisher beach house is—fabulous place,' said Martin. 'Mark's old man is pretty wealthy, you know.'

'Really? No, I didn't know,' Jane said hurriedly.

'Well are you or aren't you going out there on Sunday?' he persisted. Jane hesitated for a few seconds. 'I presume you've been invited,' said Martin.

'Well, sort of,' Jane said quietly. 'I think I was an afterthought.'

'Rubbish!' Martin exploded. 'Of course you weren't! You *must* go—they give tremendous parties.'

Jane smiled. 'I'll think about it,' was all she'd commit herself to.

'I shall expect you to be there,' said Martin, rising from the table. 'Well, I must away— duty calls. See you on Sunday, Jane.'

'Perhaps,' she said with an enigmatic smile. There were still a couple of days before she needed to make a decision.

By Saturday afternoon, Jane had come to the conclusion that it would be churlish of her not to accept the invitation simply because she had disliked the cavalier manner in which it had been given. She swallowed her pride and phoned St Margaret's, asking to speak to Dr Frobisher.

'Mark?' she said, as the familiar voice answered. 'It's Jane. I'd like to come to your parents' party tomorrow.' There was a slight pause before he replied.

'I'm so glad, Jane. My parents will be delighted to meet you—after all this time,' he added smoothly.

'Yes, well, I've just realised I don't know how to get there,' she said quietly.

'I'll send a boat. Can you be ready by eleven?'

'Yes. Things are fairly quiet here at the moment,' Jane replied.

'Good. Our boat will be in Cheung Lau harbour at eleven,' he said. 'Oh—and bring a bikini. That delicious little white number you were almost wearing at Cynthia's will do,' he added, his voice suddenly losing its cool, professional manner.

'I told you,' laughed Jane, 'I only borrowed it from Cynthia.'

'Pity—it looked fabulous *on*—probably fabulous *off*, too.' His voice trailed away at the other end, then suddenly became brisk and efficient again.

'I've got to go, someone's just come in. See you tomorrow. Goodbye.'

The phone went dead and Jane was left staring down at the desk. She put the receiver back on its cradle and continued with her weekly report, finding it extremely difficult to concentrate. Just as she was finishing, she heard footsteps on the path outside the clinic. Looking up she saw a young girl, heavily pregnant, standing in the doorway.

Jane got up from the desk and went to meet her. The girl put out a hand and grabbed Jane's, saying in rapid Cantonese, 'My baby is coming!'

'Come inside,' said Jane, gently leading her through into the treatment room. She helped her on to the treatment couch and started to examine her. The girl was rather vague when she replied to Jane's questions, but it seemed that she had been feeling contractions for some time—quite how long, it was impossible to find out.

Jane palpated the abdomen and felt a slight contraction of the uterine muscles, but there were no other signs that the arrival of the baby was imminent. She seemed to be in the early stages of labour, and would have to be admitted. Jane noted that she was a strong, healthy-looking girl, so she didn't envisage any problems.

'We shall have to admit you,' she said calmly. 'The baby's on its way, but it could be some time. Is this your first baby?' The girl nodded.

'And your husband—where is he?' asked Jane.

The girl smiled vaguely and said something about him being out on the sea somewhere.

'Will he know where you are when he gets back?' Jane asked, wishing her Cantonese was better. The girl shrugged her shoulders and stared vacantly out of the window.

'Well, we'd better get you into one of our rooms,' Jane said briskly. 'Come along with me.'

Jane went back to the phone and made a routine call to St Margaret's to say they had admitted a normal labour case and a doctor would not be required. She made a regular check on the new patient throughout the afternoon but there seemed to be no progress. The foetal heartbeat was plainly distinguishable, the baby's head was engaged, but the contractions seemed to have disappeared and there was no dilation of the birth channel.

Jane sat down in a chair beside the bed.

'What shall I call you?' she asked the girl gently.

'Mai,' replied the patient.

'Well, Mai,' explained Jane quietly. 'I think this might be a false alarm. It sometimes happens with a first baby. I don't think your baby's going to come tonight.'

The girl looked alarmed. 'He's all right, isn't he?' she asked.

'Oh, yes, of course,' said Jane with a smile, adding, 'You're sure the baby is a boy, then?'

Mai smiled. 'Yes, he's a boy,' she said happily.

'Well, we'll see,' Jane said. 'Meanwhile, I want you to get some rest. It's hard work having a baby, so try to have a good night's sleep. There's a bell here by the bed. You can ring me if you want anything.'

Jane stood up and started to leave.

'Oh, but, Sister!' Mai implored. 'Don't leave me, I don't want to be left alone! The baby might come in the night.'

Jane walked back to the bedside and took hold of Mai's hand.

'Now listen to me, Mai,' she said gently. 'If you feel the slightest pain coming on, you press that bell and I'll be with you immediately, OK?'

'No, no!' cried Mai, her voice rising to a hysterical shriek as she clung to Jane's hand. 'Don't leave me, please don't leave me.'

Jane sat down resignedly in the chair and

pressed the bell. A few seconds later Nurse Lee appeared.

'Yes, Sister?' she enquired as she came into the room.

'I'm going to stay with Mai until she's calmed down. We can't let her get upset at this point,' said Jane.

'I can stay if you like,' said Nurse Lee helpfully.

'No, you run along and take some time off. I'll ring you if I need any help. Could you bring me a book to read? There's one by the side of my bed.'

'Yes, of course, Sister.'

Nurse Lee went away and came back a few minutes later with the book. Jane settled herself in the chair, noting the grateful smile on her young patient's face as she did so. Well, that was some consolation. She tried to get comfortable, but it was rather difficult. It had been a long, hot day and the only thing she really wanted was a refreshing bath and her own cool sheets. Mai dozed fitfully, but wakened frequently to call out for her.

She's like a child, thought Jane. Strange to think that very soon she'll be a mother. She tried to concentrate on her book, but gradually felt herself drifting off into a light sleep. She dreamed she was standing by a swimming-pool in a white bikini. Someone was touching her on the shoulder. She reached up to take his hand and awoke with a start to find Nurse Lee bending over her.

'Sister, you can't stay here all night,' she was saying. 'I'll take over for a few hours.'

Outside, the night sky was like black velvet, dotted with the tiny pin points of twinkling stars.

'Good heavens, what time is it, Nurse Lee?' Jane asked sleepily.

'It's three o'clock, Sister. Go and have some rest,' said Nurse Lee.

'Thank you, I will.' Jane stood up and looked at the patient, who was sleeping peacefully. 'Wake me if you need me, Nurse Lee.'

Jane went thankfully to her room. Stripping off her uniform, she crawled between the sheets and fell asleep almost at once.

When she awoke, the sun was high in the sky. She sat up in bed quickly and looked at her watch. Nine o'clock!

After a quick shower she went along to see Mai. Nurse Lee was still sitting with her and smiled as Jane came in.

'Any change?' Jane asked.

'No. It was a false alarm,' said Nurse Lee. 'But she gets quite hysterical if I try to leave her.'

'I'll stay with her this morning,' said Jane. 'You'd better go and have some breakfast.'

'But you're going over to Sheko, Sister,' protested Nurse Lee. 'You must go and get ready. I can cope here. We'll leave Mai's door open so we can keep popping in to check up on her. She's not a child.'

'I think I'd better stay,' Jane continued dubiously.

'No,' said Nurse Lee firmly. 'Go off and enjoy yourself, Sister—you work too hard! I'll phone you if there are any developments.'

Jane examined the patient. There were absolutely no signs of labour now. She straightened up from the bed and turned to Nurse Lee.

'All right, I'll go over to Sheko. But be sure to phone if she goes into labour. I want to be here for the delivery.'

'Of course, Sister. Don't worry,' Nurse Lee smiled. 'Enjoy your day.'

Jane explained to Mai that she was going away for a few hours and would see her later in the day. 'But you will be here to deliver my baby, Sister?' she pleaded.

'Yes of course I will,' said Jane. 'Now, rest quietly and be a good girl. Nurse Lee will look after you.'

CHAPTER EIGHT

JANE walked briskly along the path towards Cheung Lau harbour. At that moment the last thing she wanted to do was to leave her patient and go out to enjoy herself.

Still, Nurse Lee has promised to phone me if there are any developments, she thought. Perhaps I have been working too hard . . . She looked around her at the wild flowers growing beside the path, and then ahead of her at the blue sea. Her mind moved on automatically to the day ahead.

Anchored in the harbour was a huge, opulent boat, which was attracting a great deal of attention from the people on the waterside. This must be the Frobisher boat, thought Jane. Sure enough, a tall young man in an immaculate white uniform stepped on shore as he saw Jane arriving.

'Sister Marshall?' he asked, holding out his hand.

'Yes, good-morning,' said Jane.

'I am to take you over to Sheko, madam,' he said courteously as he helped her on board.

'Thank you,' said Jane, looking admiringly round the luxurious boat.

'Would you care to sit below in the cabin?' he asked.

'No, no, I'm very happy here on deck, thank you.' Jane settled herself on one of the long, low sun chairs. 'I love the sea air,' she added, smiling at the helpful young man.

'A cool drink, perhaps?' he asked.

'Well, yes . . . just a fruit juice,' Jane said. She sighed contentedly and settled back on the soft cushions as the young skipper delivered brisk orders to a member of his crew.

The drink, when it arrived, was long and cold, and decorated with oriental fruit and a touch of mint. The ice-cubes clinked invitingly as Jane accepted the glass and took her first sip of the delicious concoction. By now the boat was speeding across the water, away from the congestion of Cheung Lau harbour, towards the open sea. Jane closed her eyes and luxuriated in the sheer pleasure of being pampered in such idyllic surroundings. It was only then that she realised she had worked almost nonstop for the last week. She had taken no time off duty since last Sunday—since Cynthia's party.

'If you look in this direction you can see the Frobisher beach house at Sheko.' The young man was pointing across the water to the coastline, clearly visible in the strong sunlight.

Jane shielded her eyes with one hand and, looking in the direction he was indicating, she could see a rocky coast, stretching down to a sandy beach.

'That's the Frobisher house, madam—the one on the headland,' he said helpfully.

Jane gazed in amazement at the magnificent building with its grounds jutting out to the edge of the sea.

'But I thought it was simply a beach house!' she said in a surprised voice.

He laughed. 'The Frobishers call it their beach house,' he said, 'because it's not their main house. They only use it at weekends.'

'I see,' said Jane thoughtfully, watching incredulously as the boat neared the coastline. So this was where Mark had wanted to bring her for a honeymoon eight years ago? Yes, she remembered him telling her how the sea pounded on the rocks below the house. She remembered him saying they could lie awake at night watching the moon high above the water, and listening to the roar of the waves . . .

'So this is your first visit to Sheko, madam?'

'Yes, yes it is.' Jane pulled herself together and sat up straight in the chair, swinging her long, slim legs on to the deck. 'We seem to be nearly there,' she said, suddenly feeling very nervous and hoping it didn't show. She could already distinguish a crowd of people around the swimming-pool on the headland. The boat pulled into a narrow creek and the young skipper leapt ashore to help her disembark.

'Jane!' A welcome voice called to her from the terrace. It was Martin.

Jane smiled and waved to him. 'Heavens, am I glad to see you!' she murmured as he leapt over the terrace wall and ran to meet her. 'I'd no idea it was such an enormous place.'

Martin laughed. 'Yes it's not exactly how you visualise a beach house, is it?' he said taking her arm. 'The first time I came, I was expecting to find one of those little cabins you see on the sea front at Frinton, complete with portable barbecue!'

They both laughed as they walked arm in arm through the open french doors of the house. Mark was standing in the middle of a huge reception area and came towards them, the look in his eyes showing that he had noticed their entrance together.

'So glad you could come, Jane,' he said smoothly, ignoring Martin. 'I'd like you to meet my mother.'

Jane felt her arm being taken in a firm grip, and automatically she moved away from Martin, who was left standing alone by the window. Mark propelled her briskly across the luxurious reception room to a cool terrace, shaded by enormous fronds of tropical palms. The view of the sea was breathtaking and Jane paused for a moment as they stepped out on to the terrace.

'What is it?' Mark looked at her enquiringly. 'Oh, nothing,' she said quietly. 'It's just so beautiful. It's the most beautiful house I've ever been in.'

Their eyes met for a moment and Jane looked away quickly, trying to disguise the depth of her feelings.

'Yes, it is lovely,' Mark said casually. 'Wherever I travel I always return here to recharge my batteries. It's my favourite place on earth.' He smiled gently as he looked down at her, and Jane's heart began to beat faster. There were butterflies in the pit of her stomach and her legs started to feel very weak.

Mark tightened his grip on her arm and she moved forward with him, as if in a dream. From somewhere in the dreamland she could hear Mark saying, 'Mother, this is Jane Marshall. Jane, this is my mother, Victoria Frobisher.'

The slim, elegant lady, seated at the wrought-iron table, stretched out her hand and smiled in a friendly way. She had the same beguiling charm which Mark always displayed when he liked someone.

'How do you do, Jane,' she said, shaking her hand warmly. 'Do sit down, my dear.' She indicated a vacant chair by her side, and then turning to her son she said, 'Ask someone to bring some champagne over, Mark.'

Mark started off across the terrace and

Victoria Frobisher turned back to Jane.

'Are you on the medical staff at St Margaret's?' she asked.

'I'm attached to St Margaret's, but I'm based on Cheung Lau,' Jane replied, finding it difficult to believe that this incredibly young-looking woman could be Mark's mother.

'Ah, the Cheung Lau project,' said Mrs Frobisher knowingly. 'Yes, that's very dear to my husband's heart. He's been trying to set it up for years, but it was only when he agreed to finance the whole thing that . . . Oh dear! Perhaps I shouldn't have said that, Mark doesn't like me to discuss the financial arrangements. You'd better forget it.'

'Forget what?' said Jane with a broad grin. They were both laughing together in a conspiratorial way when Mark returned with a bottle of champagne and some glasses.

'What's so funny?' he asked suspiciously.

'Nothing, dear—just women's chatter. You wouldn't understand. Why don't you make yourself useful and pour the champagne?'

'I see,' he said, looking pleased at the way they were getting on together. 'So I'm to be excluded from the conversation but allowed to exhaust myself over this champagne cork?'

'Exactly, dear.' Victoria Frobisher smiled at her son and held out her glass. There was a loud pop and the champagne flowed.

'It's funny you know, Jane, but I feel as

if I've known you a long time,' said Mrs
Frobisher. 'We haven't met before somewhere, have we?'

'No, Mother,' Mark said firmly. 'You
haven't met.'

'Well, you do seem familiar to me—but then
I would have remembered an attractive girl
like you.' She turned to her son. 'Mark, you're
not neglecting our other guests are you?'

'Mother's trying to get rid of me,' he said
with a sly wink at Jane. 'She wants to carry on
the women's talk and I'm in the way, I suppose.'

'Now just go and play host, Mark, there's a
good boy,' smiled Mrs Frobisher. 'As soon as
your father gets back he can take over. In fact,
he'll insist on taking over.'

'Your wish is my command,' he said with
mock gallantry, and kissed his mother's hand.
He was standing very close to Jane and, as if on
impulse, he lifted her hand swiftly to his lips.
Then quickly he skipped down the steps to the
pool. The gesture did not go unnoticed by Mrs
Frobisher.

'My son seems to have taken quite a liking to
you, in the short time you've been here,' she
said with a smile. 'I'm so glad he's got some
nice friends out here. There was a time when
I worried a great deal about him. He was
very unhappy in the States. I don't think he
ever really got over that young nurse at St

Catherine's. He got engaged to Cynthia for a while—we've known her family for years—but I think he was just on the rebound.'

The sound of laughter drifted up from the pool and Jane could see Mark sitting at a table, deep in conversation with Nicola Bryant. Mrs Frobisher had noticed it too.

'Now *she* seems a nice young girl,' she said to Jane. 'Mark's brought her out here a couple of times. Very pretty, don't you think?'

Jane swallowed hard. 'Yes, very pretty, Mrs Frobisher,' she said quietly.

'Oh, call me Victoria, everyone else does,' she said. 'Otherwise I feel positively ancient.'

'Not you,' laughed Jane. 'You look much too young to be Mark's mother.'

Victoria Frobisher laughed happily. 'Very sweet of you to say so, my dear. I was married very young—I wasn't a career girl like you. I sometimes wish I had had a career, but I've been too busy with husband and family. They can be time-consuming. But I'm very happy. Do you enjoy your work, Jane?'

'Yes, very much . . . Victoria.' Jane found herself pausing before she could bring herself to use Mrs Frobisher's first name. After the initial effort it came more easily to her.

'My husband will be delighted to meet you when he returns—he's had to go into Hong Kong on business. Even on Sundays he doesn't give himself a day off if there's a problem to sort out.' Victoria smiled and then lowered her voice slightly.

'Actually, I saw him putting his golf-clubs in the boot of the car early this morning, so I suspect it will be half an hour of business, followed by a round of golf.' Her tinkling laugh echoed across the terrace and Mark looked up from the poolside.

'Mother, when are you going to release Jane and let her have a swim?' he called.

'Oh, my dear, I'm so sorry,' Victoria said hurriedly. 'How thoughtless of me. I was so enjoying out little chat. Have you got a swim-suit?' she added, looking doubtfully at Jane's handbag.

'Yes, it's in here,' Jane said patting the bag.

Victoria laughed. 'It must be a very small one. You'll find towels in the changing-room. Have a good swim. I'll see you later.'

Jane stood up and walked along the terrace to the steps leading down to the pool. Mark was quick to notice and came to meet her, leaping up the steps, two at a time. She paused on the top step as he took both her hands in his. Their eyes were level with each other as he said quietly, 'Did you bring a little white bikini?'

'I tried all the big department stores,' she said with a smile, 'but they didn't have one.'

They stood transfixed for so long that Mark began to be aware of all eyes around the pool watching them. Loudly, he said, 'Come on,

Jane. The changing-room's over there—get a move on.' He turned swiftly and ran back down the steps to Nicola's table.

Jane went slowly down the steps and into the door Mark had indicated. The poolside pavilion contained an enormous tiled room with small changing-rooms, shower rooms and, in the centre, a huge jacuzzi. Jane changed quickly into the black bikini she had bought in London, before flying out to Hong Kong. It was the most expensive bikini she had ever bought and now, looking at herself in the cubicle mirror, she was glad she had taken the plunge. At the time it had seemed ridiculously extravagant to spend so much money on such a tiny amount of material.

She walked briskly out into the sunlight and was aware that Mark's eyes were immediately upon her. He had, in fact, been watching from the moment she had disappeared and now he rose from the table, leaving Nicola in mid-sentence.

'Wow!' he breathed, as he came towards her. 'You look stunning. I bet you didn't buy that on Cheung Lau.'

'You're dead right there,' Jane laughed, feeling a sensation of utter happiness flowing all over her. It was so long since she had felt like this. It was such a weird sensation. She remembered it from long, long, ago. Her head was light, her heart was full of magic. Yes, it was magic! After all these years, she recognised the signs and symptoms—she was in love!

She shivered as Mark took her hand and led her to the the pool.

'Race you,' he called. 'Do you need a head start?'

'How dare you!' she laughed. 'Maybe *you* do,' she added, giving him a playful push. As he fell into the water, she dived in and swam quickly along the pool.

'You beast,' he spluttered, as he surfaced and raced after her. He caught up with her half way down the pool and grabbed her by the legs.

'Stop!' she laughed. 'Look, I can't move—help!'

Suddenly he pulled her below the surface and his lips were on hers. She felt his strong arms around her and her body pressed against his. Their legs entwined in the depths of the water, and Jane wanted to prolong the moment forever, like a mermaid in a paradise beneath the sea . . .

They rose to the surface gasping and spluttering, and Jane could see Nicola's cold, hostile stare from the pool-side, but she didn't care any more. She was alive again. She was young and in love and nothing else mattered. They swam side by side, with gentle strokes to the end of the pool. As Jane raised her eyes above the edge she saw Martin waiting for her, attempting to keep a good-natured grin on his face. He wasn't very successful.

'Have a good swim?' he asked, unable to keep the irony out of his voice.

'Lovely,' breathed Jane, as she climbed out of the pool and shook herself.

'I believe this is madam's towel,' said Martin in a sarcastic voice, as he tossed it over to her.

'Thanks, Martin.' Jane flung it round her shoulders and started to pat herself dry.

Mark was already by her side and took the towel from her. 'Here, let me help,' he said casually.

'I thought you were going to need a life-saver out there,' Martin said coldly. 'Rather silly to stay underwater so long, I would have thought.'

'Don't worry, Martin,' said Jane coolly. 'I can take care of myself.'

'I'm sure you can,' he said, striding away towards Nicola's table.

'Thank you Mark,' Jane said. Gently taking the towel from his hands, she added under her breath, 'We seem to be the focus of attention.'

Mark grinned mischievously. 'I don't think I care, and here comes Father—I want to introduce you.'

A tall, distinguished-looking man, his hair greying at the temples, was stepping nimbly down the stairs to the poolside. He was wearing a pair of black swimming trunks and his sun-tanned, athletic body belied the fact that he was in his early sixties. As he came towards them Jane noticed the same rugged good looks, the same piercing blue eyes, the same dazzling smile. He held out his hand towards her.

'So this is the gorgeous girl in your life, Mark,' he said, his blue eyes twinkling. 'I was watching you from the terrace. How have you managed to hide her from us for so long?'

Mark looked slightly taken aback, and ignored his father's question, saying formally.

'Father, this is Jane Marshall. Jane, this is my father, Richard Frobisher.'

'How do you do . . .' began Jane, in the same formal way, but Richard Frobisher interrupted.

'Come on, you two, let's cut the formalities. It's good to see you Jane—and to see you looking so happy, Mark.' He turned round and waved to one of the servants. 'Can a man get a drink around here? I'm dying of thirst after a hard morning on the golf-course!'

Mark laughed. 'Mother said it wasn't all business this morning.'

'Shrewd woman, your mother,' he said, turning as he did so to blow a kiss towards his wife, who was watching them from the terrace. 'Come on down here, darling,' he called.

'It's too hot,' Victoria called back. 'I'll join you later, when it's cooler.'

Two of the servants had placed a table beside Mr Frobisher and were starting to pour our more champagne. Jane sat down between the two men.

'Let's have a toast,' said Richard Frobisher, raising his glass. 'To the most beautiful girl I've seen all day—besides your mother, that is.' Mark and Richard Frobisher raised their glasses, and Jane, not being sure of what she should do in this situation, sat very still and waited until the men had taken their first drink before daring to sip her own.

'You're a dark horse, Mark,' said his father genially. 'Where've you been hiding this delightful creature?'

'Father, this is Sister Marshall. She's in charge of the nursing staff at the Cheung Lau clinic.'

'Well, wonders never cease! Beautiful and intelligent too,' said Richard Frobisher. 'When I saw your curriculum vitae and heard about your successful career I didn't imagine you'd look like this. No, the Sister Marshall I imagined wasn't at all attractive—but a first-class nursing sister!'

'Father was involved in setting up the Cheung Lau project,' put in Mark, hurriedly. 'This is how he seems to know so much about your career.'

'I see,' Jane said, looking across the table at Mark and seeing him again, as if for the first time. There seemed to be an electric current running between them. Their eyes met and this time Jane did not look away. She wanted to drown herself in their blue depths, as she had wanted to submerge with him forever in the water. Oblivious to everything, Jane suddenly realised that his father was speaking to her.

'Have you seen our beach yet?' he was asking.

'The beach? No, I mean . . . only briefly, when I arrived,' she stammered.

'Mark, why don't you take Jane down there?' Richard said. 'I can look after the guests—you've done your stint this morning.'

'Thanks, Father.' Mark stood up. 'I'd like a breath of sea air. It's very hot here.'

'Yes, it's much too hot here,' Richard Frobisher said, a mischievous grin on his face. 'Go down to the sea and cool off. I'll go and join your mother on the terrace.'

'There's a short cut through here,' Mark said quietly, as he took Jane's hand and led her along a tree-lined path towards the sea, which stretched blue and inviting at the end. They walked hand in hand down the sandy beach and plunged into the cooling water, swimming quickly towards a tiny island rising out from the sea. Mark helped Jane to climb out of the water and together they lay on the warm rocks, basking in the hot sunlight. Neither of them spoke for several minutes. Then Mark took Jane's hand and pulled her to her feet.

'It's more comfortable along here,' he said, leading her to a tiny sandy cove, shaded by trees. The shore-line was still visible, but Jane felt as if they were marooned on a desert island, miles from anywhere. The world did not exist any more. There was only Mark, the sea, the sand, and this overwhelming feeling of passion welling up inside her.

He pulled her down on to the warm sand beneath the trees and his lips sought hers, gently at first and then with a hungry insistence. She responded with a passion equal to his. When she opened her eyes he was looking down at her in that heart-rending way.

'I don't understand you, Jane,' he said tenderly.

'Mark, there's something I must explain, something I've wanted to tell you ever since Cynthia's party,' she began hesitantly.

'Yes, go on,' he said gently. 'I'm listening.'

'I made a mistake,' she faltered.

'So you said the other day.' His eyes, quizzical and now worried, were searching hers.

'Mark, I honestly thought you were married to Cynthia,' she blurted out.

He burst out laughing. 'Jane, you didn't! So that explains it. Now I see!' He had stopped laughing, 'Oh, my poor love! So that was why you were giving me all that talk about only a professional relationship being possible. I just couldn't understand you.'

His voice trailed away as he took her face in his hands. She found she was crying with relief and he started to kiss the tears from her eyes, from her cheeks and then from her lips. All their pent-up feelings were released as they kissed, drowning in a mutual feeling of incredible longing. His hands touched her shoulders and she shivered in anticipation. As he held her close to him and caressed her body, she felt that the ecstasy was more than she could bear. To be here in Mark's arms again, after all those long years. She had wanted him for so long, and now . . .

His gentle hands were fondling her breasts and she felt a stirring inside her which she had never before experienced—not even in those days, long ago, when they had been young and in love for the first time. This was heaven; this was sheer bliss. She abandoned herself to his touch, to the feel of those skilful hands exploring her body . . .

From somewhere in the real world, a voice was calling across the water.

'Dr Frobisher—Dr Frobisher, sir!' It was one of the servants standing on the beach, waving frantically.

Jane started to search madly in the sand for

her bra, but Mark was fully composed. He sat up and looked across at the servant.

'What do you want?' he shouted, as if nothing had happened.

'Dr Frobisher, there is a telephone call from Cheung Lau,' the servant called. 'Sister Marshall is wanted back at the clinic.'

'How do you mean, wanted back at the clinic?' said Mark irritably.

'Let me handle this.' Jane, now fully in control of herself, ran down to the sea and called across the narrow strip of water, 'What's the problem?'

'They want you at the clinic, Sister. Your patient is going to have her baby,' yelled the servant.

'Thank you,' said Jane. 'Tell them I'll come at once.

'Hold on, a minute,' Mark said, towering angrily above her. 'I didn't know we had a difficult delivery at the clinic.'

'We haven't—it's going to be a perfectly normal birth,' said Jane easily.

'So why do you have to be there? You've got two expert nurses.'

'I promised the patient I would be there for the delivery,' Jane said quietly.

'Jane, I'll send a couple of midwives over from St Margaret's, if it'll make you feel any better,' Mark tried to persuade her. 'Just when we've got back together again . . .'

'I'm sorry,' Jane said firmly. 'It's a case of divided loyalties . . .'

'Yes,' he broke in harshly. 'And it's easy to see where your loyalties lie—and always will lie. You haven't changed a bit, Jane. Career first, last and forever. You're not flesh and blood—you're a machine!' He plunged into the water and started to swim back to the shore.

'Mark, wait!' Desperately Jane swam after the receding figure, but he reached the shore long before she did and, without a backward glance, hurried up the beach towards the house.

CHAPTER NINE

THE FROBISHER boat sped across the water towards Cheung Lau. Outwardly calm, but inwardly seething with emotion, Jane sat on the front deck, feeling the salt spray of the sea on her face and the soothing breeze ruffling her hair.

'I'm so sorry you had to cut short your visit, madam,' said the young skipper, coming up quietly beside her. 'Can I get you anything?'

'No, thank you.' Jane forced a little smile and then turned back to stare across the water. He withdrew, sensing that she wished to be alone.

The boat pulled in to Cheung Lau harbour and Jane stepped ashore. It seemed like a lifetime since she had left, and yet it was only a few hours.

She turned and walked quickly along the path towards the clinic. No need to run. A nurse never runs except in cases of fire, flood or emergency. She remembered her old sister tutor telling her that in those far-off days in the preliminary training school at St Catherine's. Well, this was neither fire, flood *nor* emergency. It was a normal delivery of a baby to a

155

healthy mother . . . but she had to be there, she had promised.

As the long, low building of the clinic came into sight she was fully composed again. Quickly she donned her white uniform and went along to the room. Nurse Lee and Nurse Wong were perfectly organised, as she had expected. The young mother, Mai, smiled happily when she saw Jane and reached for her hand.

'Sister, you came! Thank you for coming. I did so want you to be here.'

Jane smiled and the trauma of her parting at Sheko was forgotten. She took control of the situation after a brief report from her nurses. The delivery was easy and uncomplicated and an hour after Jane's arrival, Mai was holding her baby son in her arms.

'You see, I told you my baby was a boy, Sister,' she said happily. 'My husband will be so pleased.'

At the mention of the husband Jane asked Nurse Lee, 'Have we made contact with the husband yet?'

'No, Sister. He's been away for a couple of days and no one seems to know where he is.'

'He will be back soon,' said Mai calmly. 'He often goes away for a few days—then he returns. Don't worry.'

Jane smiled at the young, confident mother. 'I won't worry Mai,' she said quietly. Then, gently removing the baby from his mother's arms, she added, 'Now you must get some rest.'

When the baby was settled in his cot at the foot of the bed, Jane went along to see the other patients. Mr Peng, the chronic bronchitic, seemed to be comfortable. Jane sounded his chest; it was still in a bad state but there was an improvement in his general condition. Obviously the rest and nursing care were helping him recover.

Jane moved on to see Carol, who was sitting by the window reading. She looked up from her book and smiled delightedly when Jane came in.

'Sister, how nice to see you! They told me you'd gone away for the day.'

'I was called back,' said Jane. 'We've got an addition to the family—just along the corridor. It's a boy.'

'I thought I heard a baby crying,' said Carol. 'Is everything OK?'

'Fine. No complications and mother and baby are thriving,' Jane said with a smile.

'Hope it didn't spoil your day, Sister—I mean, having to leave the party early,' said Carol.

'No, no, not at all,' Jane said hurriedly. Then, quickly putting on her professional voice, she added, 'Stitches out tomorrow, Carol.'

Carol pulled a face. 'And then what, Sister?'

'And then back into the big, wide world again, my girl,' said Jane, grinning broadly.

Carol lay back in the chair and pretended to look ill. 'Oh Sister, I feel so weak,' she said, in a caricature of a dying patient.

'Yes, I don't think you'll last the night.' Jane smiled, going along with the tragic drama. 'However, if you do, I'll take your stitches out. And then perhaps, if you're a really good girl, you can stay until Tuesday. But then I turn you out.'

Carol beamed all over her face and dropped the dramatic performance. 'Oh, thank you, Sister. You're so kind,' she said. 'And, you see, I've got to finish this book before I go.'

Jane laughed. 'Well, if that's all that's worrying you, you can always take the book with you. I shall want to keep a check on you, so you'll have to keep coming back to out-patients, you know.'

'Oh will I? That's nice.' Carol returned to her book and Jane went out on to the veranda. It had been a long day. The sun was beginning to set behind the hill, casting a red glow over the green fields, the yellow sand and the blue sea. The air was cool now and everything was calm and quiet. Even the birds had stopped singing. She found herself wondering what was happening across the water at Sheko. Would the guests have gone home, or would some of them still be sitting out on the terrace with the Frobisher family, enjoying the sunset over Hong Kong? And if she had stayed, instead of returning here to Cheung Lau, what would have happened?

She shivered at the thought and forced herself to think only of the work in hand. Tomorrow would be a busy day and she must get some rest.

Early the next day, Jane was awakened by a loud knocking at the main door. Hurriedly she slipped on her robe and went to see who it was. Peering through the small glass window, she could see a young man standing on the step outside. Mai's husband, she thought hopefully, as she slid back the huge bolts and unlocked the door.

'Where is she?' the young man asked abruptly. 'My wife—where is she?'

'If you mean Mai Ling, she's safely tucked up in bed,' said Jane. 'I presume you are the husband who's been missing for a few days?'

'Yes, yes,' he said breathlessly. 'I came as soon as I got back to shore. They told me she was here. Is she well? Can I see her?' His words tumbled out in a rush of anxiety and Jane began to feel sorry for this young, inexperienced father. She glanced at the clock in the reception room—four o'clock.

'I'd rather you wait until morning. Your wife is very tired,' she said gently. 'You have a beautiful baby boy.' The young man's face creased into a smile of delight.

'A boy!' he breathed. 'Oh, I did so want a son—someone to help me with my fishing.'

Jane smiled. 'He's a little young for that yet, but no doubt he'll grow.'

'And is Mai fit and healthy?' he asked. 'Will she have other sons?'

'I've no doubt she'll have many sons,' said Jane drily. 'But at the moment, all she needs is rest. You can have a peep at your wife and baby, but you mustn't wake them if they are asleep.'

He followed Jane along the corridor and through to Mai's room. Jane opened the door quietly, but when Mai heard it she awoke. Her husband bounded through the door like a young schoolboy and made straight for the bed. Mai smiled happily as he kissed her gently. Then he went to the foot of the bed and stared, wide-eyed, at the sleeping baby.

'Is this him?' he said nervously, pointing at the tiny bundle.

'Of course it is,' laughed Mai. 'Who else could it be?'

'My son,' breathed the young man, and before Jane could stop him he had picked up the tiny baby and was cradling him lovingly in his arms.

'He's so small,' he said in amazement.

Jane and Mai laughed. 'Of course he's

small,' said Jane. 'So were you at his age. Now, do you think he could be allowed to sleep on a little longer? He might decide he's hungry if you wake him.'

'Yes, yes of course, Sister.' The young father placed the precious bundle back in his cot and went back to his wife. Jane went out on to the veranda so that they could be alone together for a few minutes. After all, they must have so much to talk about, she thought. The sun was rising out of the water beyond the harbour, casting an eerie glow over the boats anchored there. The people on board were coming to life and the whole of the waterfront was beginning to stir with activity.

Might as well start my day too, thought Jane. No point in trying to go back to sleep.

When the young father had gone, she went along to her room, showered and put on a clean uniform. She could have everything prepared before Cynthia arrived for the day's clinic. There was her report to write, the treatment sheets to bring up to date. So much to do, she told herself. So much to do, and no time to think about myself. That's good—just how I like it. When Nurse Lee came on duty she was surprised to see Jane sitting at the desk, finishing off her report.

'Did you have to get up early, Sister?' she asked.

'Yes. Mai's husband arrived about four.

Didn't you hear the noise? He was banging on the door for ages,' said Jane.

'No, I didn't hear a thing,' said Nurse Lee. 'I sleep very soundly—nothing wakes me.'

'You're lucky,' said Jane wistfully. 'I used to, but recently I find I sleep only fitfully. I don't know why—perhaps it's the heat.'

She paused and looked at Nurse Lee. 'You look fresh and ready for action this morning, Nurse. Will you go in and wash Mai, and then bath the baby. Nurse Wong can take care of Mr Peng. I'm going to remove Carol's stitches.'

She stood up from her desk and went briskly over to the treatment room to collect her instruments. Carol was surprised to see Sister arriving bright and early with a surgical tray. She had been lingering over her breakfast and had barely finished when Jane went in.

'Come on, Carol,' Jane said, a trifle sharply. Then, remembering that the rest of the world did not share her passion for work, she modified her tone and said gently, 'I thought you would have finished your breakfast ages ago.'

'I'm enjoying my last day as a lady of leisure,' said Carol mischievously. Then, looking at the surgical tray, she added, 'Will it hurt, Sister?'

'Of course it won't hurt,' Jane said brusquely. 'I've taken out more stitches than I care to remember, and I've never lost a patient yet.'

'Well, that's very comforting,' said Carol with a grin, settling back on her pillows as she watched Jane scrubbing her hands at the sink.

When the dressing had been removed, Jane scrubbed up again before deftly snipping and removing the sutures.

'The wound has healed beautifully,' she said to Carol. 'There'll be absolutely no scar in a few months.'

'That's good, because I'm planning on going on a world-cruise and I shall lie topless in the sunshine,' said Carol with a wry grin. Jane looked carefully at the young girl and sensed the anxiety beneath the brash exterior.

'Seriously, Carol, what *are* you going to do when you leave here?'

Carol shrugged her shoulders. 'No idea,' she said with an attempt at indifference which didn't fool Jane.

'You're an intelligent girl,' said Jane. 'Have you tried to get a job?'

'Sometimes. Now and then I've tried, but there isn't much I can do,' she said quietly.

'You can read and write, which is more than lots of people can do,' said Jane. 'And how about domestic work—have you tried that?'

'Well, actually, I was wondering . . .' Carol started, then paused.

'Yes, go on. You were wondering what?'

'I was wondering if you need any help in the kitchen,' she blurted out.

Jane laughed. 'How long have you been thinking that one out?' she asked.

'Well, I was lying here and I thought to myself, wouldn't it be nice to work here. And as I've got no qualifications whatsoever, maybe they'd take me on as a cleaner or something,' said Carol, watching Jane's face intently.

'Look, I'll have a word with the powers that be, and we'll see what we can do,' Jane said. 'I expect Mary could do with an extra pair of hands in the kitchen, but I can't promise anything. Anyway, I'll do my best.'

'Thanks, Sister, you're a marvel,' said Carol happily.

Jane smiled at her, picked up the tray and went off to the treatment room. Nurse Wong was sterilizing instruments and preparing the treatment couches.

'How's Mr Peng?' asked Jane.

'Improving all the time,' replied Nurse Wong, efficiently continuing with his work. 'He's had a good night and seems comfortable. Dr Martin is here, Sister. She's already started the clinic.'

'Really? She's an early bird today.' Jane went through into the reception room to find Cynthia seated at the main desk and deep in conversation with a patient.

'You're very early today, Cynthia,' she said, with a smile.

'Apparently so were you, by all accounts,' replied Cynthia, her eyes searching Jane's face. 'I came over early so we could have a chat, but they tell me you've been hard at it since the crack of dawn. What's the matter—couldn't you sleep?'

'Of course I could sleep,' Jane said quickly. 'I got woken up at four by a young father demanding to see his new son. There didn't seem much point in going back to bed after that.'

'I'm worried about you,' said Cynthia. 'You look tired today.'

'I'm fine,' Jane said quickly. 'Shall I fetch the next patient?'

'Yes please.' Cynthia leaned back in her chair and watched the retreating figure thoughtfully.

They took a coffee-break in the middle of the morning and Cynthia tried again to make Jane talk.

'Sorry we missed you at Sheko yesterday,' she said innocently. 'Dave and I were held up and by the time we arrived you'd gone.'

'Yes, I had to come back to deliver Mai's baby,' Jane said quietly, as she sipped her coffee.

'Oh, what was the problem?' asked Cynthia.

'No problem—I'd just promised to be there,

that's all,' Jane explained lightly.

'Pity. I expected to see you and Mark enjoying yourselves at long last,' said Cynthia. She added cautiously, 'Instead, there he was with that scatty young blonde nurse—what's her name?'

'Nicola Bryant,' Jane supplied quietly.

'That's the one. She's the one who was chasing him at my party, wasn't she? Jane I really think . . .' Cynthia broke off in mid-sentence as Nurse Lee came in and helped herself to coffee.

'Everything all right with the mother and baby?'

'Fine, Sister. Both doing well,' Nurse Lee assured them.

'Will you see the in-patients now or at the end of the morning, Doctor?' Jane asked Cynthia.

'I'll come along now, I think,' said Cynthia, putting her coffee-cup down on the table. 'Let me see. Who've we got in now, Sister?'

'We've got a mother and baby in room one, a chronic bronchitic in room two and a removal of benign tumour in room three—you remember Carol, who came over to St Margaret's?'

'Yes, I remember her. How is she?' Cynthia asked.

'In excellent health. I removed the stitches this morning,' Jane said. 'Her main problem is finding a job and somewhere to live when we discharge her tomorrow. Do you think we could take her on in the kitchen?'

'I don't see why not,' said Cynthia. 'Why don't you ask Mark?'

'I'd rather you ask him, when you get back today,' Jane muttered hurriedly.

Cynthia gave her a quizzical look. 'OK then, if that's what you want. I'm sure he'll agree.'

'Good. You'll let me know, Cynthia?'

'Yes, yes of course. I'll ring you when I've spoken to Mark,' Cynthia said, hiding her surprise. 'Lead the way, Sister.'

She asked Jane no further questions about Mark. If she sensed that something was wrong she had obviously decided it was now beyond her control. When she left the clinic at midday she promised to let Jane know about Carol's job as soon as possible.

'Thank you Cynthia. That would be a great help,' said Jane. 'I'd like to see her settled. She's a bright girl—just had a difficult time, that's all.'

'Yes, of course,' said Cynthia. 'Don't worry about her. I'm sure the answer will be yes. The Frobishers are very philanthropic people,' she added with a smile.

'So it would seem,' said Jane, in a neutral voice.

Later in the afternoon, when Nurse Wong came to say there was a phone call from St

Margaret's for her, Jane felt sure that it would be Cynthia. The masculine voice at the other end of the phone was the last thing she expected to hear.

'Dr Frobisher here,' he said impersonally. 'I understand you'd like to employ an ex-patient in the kitchen?'

'Yes, that's correct,' confirmed Jane determined to be equally cool. 'It's Carol. You operated on her last . . .'

'Yes, I know all the medical details, Sister,' he interrupted irritably. 'The important thing is, do you think she's honest and trustworthy?'

'From what I've seen of her she seems . . .'

Again, Mark interrupted her. 'From what you've seen of her you would recommend her, then?'

'Yes, I would,' Jane said firmly, at last beginning to get her breath back.

'That's all I wanted to hear,' he said, in the same cold, neutral voice. 'She may have the job. Perhaps you could arrange accommodation with your cook, Sister.'

'Yes, Doctor,' Jane replied mechanically.

The phone went dead. The interview was over. Apparently it was *all* over—even before it started. Jane shook herself out of her sudden lethargy and went to tell Carol the good news. At least she'd made one person happy today.

She felt very tired during the next few days and had to force herself to work with her usual efficiency. It must be the heat, she thought, or perhaps I'm sickening for something. When Martin came to take the clinic on Thursday he expressed his concern at her appearance.

'Jane, what are you doing to yourself? You look terrible,' he said.

'Thanks, Martin,' said Jane in a flat, lifeless voice. 'You're a great help to a girl's flagging morale!'

'Look, I insist you take a day off tomorrow. We can't have you going around looking half-dead. It's bad for the patients,' he joked. 'What you need is a whole day away from it all. I'll take you out in my boat and make a new woman of you.'

'Oh, Martin, you know I can't . . .' she began, but he cut her short.

'There's no such thing as can't,' he said firmly. 'Doctor's orders! Nurse Lee, is there any reason why Sister shouldn't take a day off tomorrow?'

'Of course not, Dr Chandler,' Nurse Lee replied. 'It will do her good. I've told her she works too hard.'

'That's settled then. Ten o'clock sharp at Cheung Lau harbour—and I won't take no for an answer.'

'You talked me into it,' Jane smiled. 'I'm too tired to argue with you, if the truth be known.'

Saying this, she retreated into the treatment

room and hoped everyone would stop fussing about her health.

At ten o'clock the next morning she found herself standing on the quayside carrying a canvas bag which contained a bikini, a towel and a cooked chicken—which Mary had insisted she take in case the dear Dr Chandler had forgotten to pack a picnic! His boat was just pulling into the harbour as she arrived, and he leapt off on to the waterside and gave her a welcoming kiss on the cheek.

'Jane, you look lovely,' he complimented her sincerely. 'A trifle peaky, perhaps, and your sun-tan needs touching up, but just leave it all to Uncle Martin.'

Jane laughed—the first time for days. It was difficult not to feel cheerful when Martin was around. He took her bag and helped her on to the boat. Noticing the weight of the bag, he raised his eyebrows. 'What's this? Goodies?'

'I'm afraid so! Mary insisted I bring a chicken, just in case.'

'But I told you *I* would bring the food! There's enough for a banquet now,' he laughed. 'I'll stash it away in the cold box.'

Martin pulled out of Cheung Lau using the outboard motor, and then put the sails up as soon as they were clear of the harbour. There was a fair breeze and the boat sailed along merrily, the sails flapping above them. Jane stretched out on one of the benches and allowed Martin to do all the work. He seemed very happy to be in command and called out, 'Now don't you lift a finger unless I tell you to, young lady! This is your day of rest.'

'Aye, aye, captain!' said Jane, closing her eyes against the strong sunlight. They were tacking out towards the open sea and there was a pleasant, cooling breeze. When she opened her eyes Martin was standing beside her with a glass of fruit juice.

'Drink this,' he said, unceremoniously thrusting the glass into her hand. She took a sip of the cold drink and pulled a face.

'Martin, this isn't just fruit juice, is it?'

He made no reply but watched her with a smile on his face. She took another sip.

'It's got something in it! Wait a minute, I know what it is,' she said. 'It's rum!'

'Just a noggin,' he admitted playfully. 'Well, we are out on the ocean waves. It'll bring the colour back into those pale, wan cheeks.'

'I do believe you're intent on having your evil way with me,' she grinned, sipping the drink nevertheless. It gave her a warming feeling in the pit of her stomach and she felt the strength flowing back into her body.

'I do believe you're right,' he said, with an attempt at a wicked smile. He sat down on the seat beside her and they sipped their drinks companionably as the boat sailed smoothly over the gentle waves.

'I'd better adjust the sails,' he decided suddenly. 'We're going to that little island over there. Here, take the rudder.'

After a few moments, Jane managed to steer the boat while Martin adjusted the sails. Soon they were on course for the tiny verdant island.

'What a superb place for a picnic,' said Jane, happily digging her toes into the soft sand. 'Do you bring all your captive maidens here?'

'Of course,' Martin said, with a wicked laugh. 'I have my evil way with them and then I bury them over there in the sand.'

'Must be quite exhausting for you,' Jane sympathised.

'Oh, it is, so let's have another noggin.' He sank down on the sand beside her and poured out two more glasses of the lethal brew.

This time Jane found she was enjoying the taste—but the effect was catastrophic. She had never felt so light-headed. The strong feeling in her arms seemed to have gone and instead they felt limp and useless. She lay back on the sand and, closing her eyes, fell asleep.

When she awoke she found Martin lying beside her. She rubbed her eyes quickly.

'Martin, how long have I been asleep?' she asked.

'Too long,' he moaned. 'I think that second drink must have knocked you out cold. I've been waiting for you to wake up, so that I could take you in my arms . . .'

He moved towards her on the sand and put his arms around her. She stiffened and lay very still.

'Martin, don't,' she said quietly but firmly. 'Please take your hands away.'

Reluctantly he pulled himself from her and sat up, looking down at her. 'The ice maiden,' he said softly. 'Or are you made of stone?'

'Don't say that,' she said, feeling the tears pricking behind her eyes. Suddenly the floodgates burst and she sobbed uncontrollably. This time she didn't stop him when he took her in his arms. She leaned her head on his chest and found comfort in the strength of his body. He made no attempt to kiss her, but simply remained with his arms around her while she sobbed as if her heart would break.

'Jane, darling, I think I know what's the matter,' he said gently. 'But I could make you happy, if only you could forget.'

'Martin, I don't want to talk about it,' she broke in, dabbing frantically at her eyes and only succeeding in smearing the tears across her cheeks in the attempt.

Martin grinned at her good-naturedly. 'Well, I must say, you do look a mess! I bring you all this way for a rest-cure and what do you do? First you pass out on me, then you play the last scene from *Traviata*. For goodness' sake woman, get into your bikini and we'll go and wash the tears away in the sea.'

'Oh, Martin, you're such a good friend.' She smiled through her tears.

'Yes, I know,' he said drily. 'Come on, get a move on.'

For the rest of the day neither of them referred to the incident. They swam for a long time before their picnic and then lay on the sand, dozing together afterwards. As they sailed home the sun was beginning to set over Hong Kong. The peak was ablaze with an orange glow of fire. They could see the twinkling lights of the big city lighting up everywhere. The boat sailed on towards Cheung Lau and into the harbour.

Martin tied it up and walked Jane back to the clinic. They stood outside the main door.

'I won't ask you in for coffee,' Jane said. 'I'm exhausted, but I've enjoyed myself, Martin. Thanks a lot. It's been a super day and you were wonderful.'

He grinned genially. 'If ever you need a friend . . .'

'Thanks, Martin, I'll remember,' she said quietly.

'I mean it, Jane. Look, here's my card. My phone number's on it. Ring me whenever you feel like it.'

Jane smiled gently at him as she took the

card. He bent down and kissed her briefly on the cheek.

'Goodnight, Jane,' he said wistfully.

'Goodnight, Martin.' She turned and went in through the door, closing it firmly behind her.

CHAPTER TEN

JANE wakened early again on Saturday morning. She lay very still in bed, thinking about her day out with Martin. He was such a kind friend—so thoughtful. She picked up his card from where it lay on her bedside table and memorised the phone number, just in case. The sun was already streaming in through the windows, so she leapt out of bed, showered, and put on her uniform.

After her day off she was beginning to feel that she was out of touch with the patients. She peeped in at the mother and baby. They were both sleeping peacefully, so she didn't disturb them. Mr Peng was also in a deep slumber— Jane could hear his loud snoring from outside the door, so she continued along the corridor to the dining-room.

There was an inviting aroma of coffee coming from the kitchen and when Jane poked her head round the door she saw Carol sitting in a chair by the window, reading. She jumped up when she saw Jane.

'Sister! I didn't expect to see you up so early,' she exclaimed.

Jane smiled at her. 'And I didn't expect to

see you around at the crack of dawn either. But I'm glad you're here, because I'm dying for a cup of coffee.'

'Yes, of course, Sister,' Carol said hurriedly. 'I'll bring it in for you.'

'No, don't bother,' Jane said. 'I'll just sit here with you.' She pulled up a chair to the kitchen table. Carol poured out two cups of coffee and joined her.

'Delicious coffee,' said Jane, after the first sip. 'How are you getting on?'

'I'm enjoying it. Mary's teaching me to cook and in my spare time I'm working my way through all the books you've got here,' Carol said happily.

'Yes, you like reading, don't you?' Jane mused thoughtfully.

'I was wondering, Sister . . . could I borrow some of your nursing books—I mean just the first stages, to see if I could understand them?' she asked shyly.

'Are you interested in nursing, Carol?'

She nodded enthusiastically. 'I wish I had the qualifications to train as a nurse,' she said wistfully.

'Well, you could work towards getting them, if that's what you really want to do,' Jane said encouragingly.

'Oh, do you think I could?' Carol's eyes shone with excitement.

'Of course. There's nothing a girl can't do

these days if she sets her mind to it. I'll get the details of the pre-nursing course in Hong Kong and we can send you over there on a day-release scheme,' said Jane efficiently.

'Thank you so much! That would be marvellous. Now, can I get you some breakfast, Sister?'

'Yes, I suppose I'd better eat something—just toast, Carol, and some more of your delicious coffee.'

Jane was still sitting at the kitchen table drinking coffee when Mary came in. She started to berate Carol in Cantonese, obviously disapproving of the fact that Jane was not being served in the dining-room.

'It's all right, Mary,' Jane said easily. 'I asked Carol if I could sit here. She makes delicious coffee.'

Mary was appeased and smiled amiably at the two of them. Jane stood up. 'Thanks for the breakfast, Carol. Keep up the good work.'

Carol smiled happily and started to busy herself with her kitchen chores, under the watchful eye of Mary. Meanwhile, Jane spent the day catching up with the normal nursing routine. She even found time to spend a couple of hours out in the garden during the afternoon. When the patients were settled in the evening, she sat on the veranda outside her bedroom. It was very quiet and peaceful. She had given Nurse Lee and Nurse Wong the night off, so they had gone over to the bright lights of Hong Kong.

Saturday night in Hong Kong, she thought. So different from this calm little island. There was not a sound in the garden, except for the droning of the insects. The sun had set, and the magic of the twilight enveloped the hillside.

I love this place, she thought. I enjoy my work. So why do I feel so sad tonight? How can I get rid of this awful dragging feeling inside me? She shivered and stood up quickly. Sleep, that's what I need, she told herself. Tomorrow, everything will seem brighter. Tomorrow, and tomorrow, and so on forever, becoming more and more efficient, more and more useful, more and more like a machine . . . She switched her thoughts abruptly and went inside.

The little room seemed cool after the heat of the day, and Jane lay down thankfully between the crisp sheets. Although she felt tired she found it impossible to sleep. Her brain was too active; her mind kept revolving round all the things that had happened to her since her arrival in Hong Kong, particularly her meeting with Mark at St Margaret's—so unexpected, after all those years of thinking he was married and living in the States. It was her second chance, her last chance, and she'd thrown it away again.

Suddenly, as if in a dream, she heard a loud

knocking at the main door. She looked at her watch—it was midnight. Not a patient at this time of night, she thought wearily as she reached for her robe.

She reached the front door and slid back the bolts. Standing on the step was a young girl in obvious pain.

'Help me, please help me!' said the girl faintly, and collapsed into Jane's arms. Fortunately she was very light, and Jane was able to lift her on to a trolley which was standing by the door. She wheeled her carefully into the treatment room, by which time the girl had opened her eyes again. She reached out a hand and took hold of Jane's, squeezing it tightly.

'I'm in such pain,' she muttered. 'Help me, please, help me.'

'Where does it hurt, my dear?' asked Jane, concerned that she was on her own.

'Here, just here—and here.' The girl was holding her hands over her abdomen.

Jane pressed very gently and could feel a hard, tender mass in the lower abdomen. She palpated the appendix area, but that seemed to be normal. The patient was sweating profusely and Jane could see that her temperature was abnormally high, even before she reached for a thermometer. The pulse rate was excessive, too.

Jane's mind began to search for a diagnosis.

She had a suspicion which she wanted to check out.

'How long is it since you had a period?' she asked the girl.

The girl looked puzzled. 'I don't know. I forget—perhaps three months.'

That was it; Jane was fairly sure of her diagnosis now, but only an operation would confirm it, and only an operation would save the girl. It was likely to be an ectopic pregnancy. The fertilized egg had started to develop inside a Fallopian tube instead of the uterus, causing swelling and intense pain. If the Fallopian tube were to burst before they could operate, the whole of the abdomen would be affected and peritonitis could set in.

Jane reached for a syringe and gave the girl a shot of pethidine to ease the pain. 'When did you have your last meal?' she asked, thinking ahead to the necessary operation.

'Oh, I don't know. Yesterday, I think,' replied the girl, weakly. 'I've been feeling so awful I . . .'

'Yes, yes, of course. Now I want you to lie still. I'm going to phone the doctor.' Jane hurried into the reception room. She had already decided which doctor. Martin would fly over at once. His number was already memorised, already in her head. She picked up the phone and dialled his flat. The courteous voice which replied belonged to his servant.

'I want to speak to Dr Chandler,' she said urgently.

'I'm afraid Dr Chandler is at a dinner party at Dr Weston's house,' replied the servant. 'Can I take a message?'

Jane's heart sank. Who on earth was Dr Weston? Oh, yes—Cynthia's husband, Dave.

'Can you phone him for me?' she asked hurriedly.

'Of course, madam,' came the polite reply.

'Ask him to fly out to Cheung Lau clinic immediately, and bring an anaesthetist. We shall have to operate at once.'

'Very good, madam,' replied the servant, calmly. 'May I have your name please?'

'Oh, yes, of course. I'm Sister Marshall.'

'Thank you, Sister. I'll ring the doctor immediately. Goodbye.'

Jane went back to the treatment room. Her patient was dozing fitfully on the couch. She could leave her for a few minutes while she prepared the small operating-theatre.

She pushed open the doors and began to feel nervous. This would be the first time the theatre had been used. Although she had checked the equipment every day since her arrival, she still had to be sure that everything worked. She scrubbed her hands and put on a theatre-gown and gloves, then methodically

set out the instruments for a salpingectomy—
excision of the affected Fallopian tube. There
was everything there which would be required,
if her diagnosis was correct. She added further
instruments, in case a general exploration of
the abdomen was necessary.

The minutes ticked by. Jane returned to the
treatment room where her patient was now
moaning quietly, still in pain, but somewhat
eased by the pethidine.

Pray God, Martin comes soon, thought
Jane. How long had it been since she'd rung?
Half an hour? She went into reception, picked
up the phone, and dialled Martin's number.
The servant answered, almost at once.

'Yes, I have rung Dr Chandler, Sister,' he
replied patiently. 'There has been a slight
problem, but Dr Frobisher is handling it.'

'Problem? What do you mean, a slight problem?' Jane asked, unable to keep the anxiety
from her voice. 'Oh, it doesn't matter, I
can hear the helicopter now. Thank you.
Goodbye.'

She put the phone down and looked out of
the window. The helicopter had just touched
down. In the bright moonlight she could see
two figures running across to the main door.
She went quickly to meet them and stopped
short in the doorway. The first to arrive was
Mark, followed closely by Dave Weston.

'Where's the patient?' Mark asked

brusquely, pushing past her.

'She . . . she's in the treatment room,' stammered Jane, as she hurried to catch up with him.

'Diagnosis?' he snapped at her.

'I suspect it's an ectopic.'

Mark's skilful hands were already palpating the abdomen. The young girl winced and cried out. Quietly, Jane gave Mark the details of the case.

'I think you could be right,' he said briefly. 'Certainly, we need to take a look. Is the theatre ready?'

'Of course,' Jane replied.

'Dave, check the anaesthetic equipment,' said Mark, marching towards the tiny anteroom. 'Sister, come and help me scrub up. I hope you've got everything we need.'

Jane drew a deep breath and followed behind Mark.

'What happened to Martin?' she dared to ask, casually, when she had finally encased the great man in his gown and mask.

Mark gave a short, sharp laugh. 'He was rather the worse for wear—drank too much at dinner, so I said I'd come. OK, Sister, let's go.'

He swept into the small operating-theatre with all the panache of a surgeon in a large teaching hospital. Jane could almost imagine the gasps of admiration from the spectators in the gallery. She turned quietly. 'You can bring the patient in now, Dr Weston.'

Dave Weston positioned himself at the head of the operating-table. Jane stood at the other side of the patient, waiting with bated breath for Mark's instructions.

'Scalpel,' he said brusquely.

Deftly she handed over the instrument. The first incision was made and the operation was under way. Mark quickly located the Fallopian tube. It was grossly distended and ready to burst at any moment.

'Your diagnosis was correct, Sister,' he said briefly, as he excised the tissue. 'Swab, please.'

Jane noted the polite request at the end of his command. I must be back in favour again, she thought drily.

'Everything OK at your end, Dave?' asked Mark.

'Fine,' came the reply. 'No problems. Well-equipped little theatre, isn't it?'

'Not bad,' said Mark, concentrating on the patient. 'Good thing we caught this when we did. Another hour or so and I dread to think what a mess it would have been. As it is, the surrounding tissues are unaffected. Sutures, Sister,' he barked, returning to his 'important-surgeon' voice. Jane handed them over and watched admiringly as the skilful hands sewed up the wound.

'There,' he said, and stood back, as if to admire his handiwork. 'We'll put her on anti-

biotics. I don't envisage any problems now.'
He looked across at Jane, as if noticing her for
the first time.

'Well done, Sister,' he said gently. Their
eyes met across the table.

'Yes, as machines go, I function quite well,'
she said quietly.

'Jane . . .' Mark started to say—then, remembering where they were, he stopped.

There was a long silence and Dave was the
first to break it. 'I'll stay with the patient until
she comes round. Perhaps you two would like
to take a break.'

'Thanks, Dave. I certainly would,' said
Mark. 'Call us when you need us.'

'Sure thing.' Dave busied himself with the
anaesthetic apparatus. 'Don't go too far away,
mind.'

'Don't worry,' Jane said. 'We'll be right next
door.'

She opened the doors and went through into
the treatment room.

'Isn't there somewhere we can cool off?'

'Well, it's probably cooler on the veranda.'
Jane, pushed wide the windows and stepped
outside. She could sense that Mark was right
behind her as she leaned against the rail. He
inched to one side and stood beside her, looking across the moonlit garden.

'Why did you send for Martin?' he asked
quietly.

'Because . . . because he's been very kind to me, and I'm very fond of him,' she replied quickly.

'Fond?' he queried.

'Yes, *fond*,' she repeated firmly, not daring to look at him.

'Nothing more?' he asked quietly.

'As if you cared,' she snapped back.

'Jane, I do care. You know I do.' He was standing much too close to her now. She could feel the warmth of his body next to hers.

'Hey, you two! Can somebody come and give me a hand in here?' Dave called.

Immediately, Jane hurried back into the treatment room. Whatever happened, her main concern had to be for the patient.

'She's coming round,' said Dave. 'Have you got a room we can transfer her to?'

'Yes, room three is empty. This way, please.' They settled the patient in bed and then Jane suggested the two men went off in search of coffee.

'Not for me,' said Dave. 'Keeps me awake. Besides, I'd like to get back to the little woman.'

'I think I'd better stay on for a while,' Mark said smoothly. 'Just in case.'

'Of course,' said Dave, with a sly wink. 'I think you should stay. Goodnight all.'

The patient was sleeping peacefully as the helicopter rose overhead. Jane and Mark went out on to the veranda. They saw its lights twinkling in the sky before it disappeared in the direction of Hong Kong.

There was a sound of footsteps on the path and in the moonlight Jane saw Nurse Lee returning. Jane waved and she came along the veranda.

'What's happened?' she asked anxiously, surprised at all the activity.

'We had to use the theatre for the first time,' said Jane. 'It was an ectopic pregnancy. Dr Frobisher came over just in time.'

'Sister sent for me just in time,' interrupted Mark, smiling. 'Nurse Lee, do you think you could stay with the patient for a short while? There's something I want to discuss with Sister.'

'Yes, of course, Doctor.' Nurse Lee was already inside the patient's room.

'The treatment sheet is at the foot of the bed,' began Jane, but Mark's arm was firmly on hers.

'Nurse Lee is perfectly capable of dealing with a post-operative patient,' he said firmly, as he steered her along the veranda.

'Mark, where are you taking me?' she asked breathlessly.

'Which is your room?' he asked bluntly.

'Mark, I don't know what you have in mind, but I want to make it perfectly clear . . .'

'Shut up, woman. Is this it?' he said, pausing

outside her window. 'Yes, of course it is,' he added quietly. 'I could recognise your room anywhere.' He stepped inside and looked around him. 'It's got the same warm, soft, feminine . . .'

'Stop it, Mark!' said Jane angrily. He wheeled round to face her, as she cried, 'How dare you force your way in here and talk about me being soft and warm? I'm only a machine, according to you—remember?'

'Oh, my darling!' His strong arms were round her in a flash. 'I didn't mean it. But I've loved you for so long—I've waited for you for so long, and you've always put your career first. Last Sunday, when it happened again, I felt I couldn't take any more. But you see, we *can* work as a team—we *can* work together! There's no need for you to make a choice between marriage and career. Don't you see, my darling? You can have both. Dave and Cynthia seem to manage OK.'

'Mark Frobisher, is this a proposal?' Jane tried to remain calm.

'Of course it is, you little goose,' he said with a grin. 'And this time I won't take no for an answer.'

'My mother always said you can't have your cake and eat it,' Jane smiled primly.

'Your mother is responsible for you making the wrong decision eight years ago,' he retorted, adding in a gentle voice, 'Of course you can have your cake and eat it. Just you wait and see . . .'

His expert fingers were untying the bows at the back of her theatre-gown. She felt shivers of anticipation running over her as they fell back on to the bed.

'Mark, wait,' she cried. 'If you loved me so much, why didn't you get in touch with me before?'

'I didn't think I'd stand a chance against your brilliant career,' he murmured. 'Oh, yes, I've followed it all the way. Then, when my father had this idea about starting a clinic on Cheung Lau, I insisted there must be a capable Sister from St Catherine's in charge. It just so happens that one of my friends happened to be on the appointments board.'

'You scheming so-and-so,' breathed Jane. 'So that was . . .'

'I thought fate needed a helping hand in bringing us together again,' he said with a wry grin. 'Are you angry with me?'

Jane smiled. 'Angry with you?' she echoed. 'With myself perhaps—but not with you.'

'We've wasted so much time,' he said, as he took her in his arms.

'Then let's not waste any more,' she murmured as his lips came down upon hers.

4 Doctor Nurse Romances
FREE

Coping with the daily tragedies and ordeals of a busy hospital, and sharing the satisfaction of a difficult job well done, people find themselves unexpectedly drawn together. Mills & Boon Doctor Nurse Romances capture perfectly the excitement, the intrigue and the emotions of modern medicine, that so often lead to overwhelming and blissful love. By becoming a regular reader of Mills & Boon Doctor Nurse Romances you can enjoy EIGHT superb new titles every two months plus a whole range of special benefits: your very own personal membership card, a free newsletter packed with recipes, competitions, bargain book offers, plus big cash savings.

**AND an Introductory FREE GIFT for YOU.
Turn over the page for details.**

**Fill in and send this coupon back today
and we'll send you**
4 Introductory
Doctor Nurse Romances yours to keep
FREE

At the same time we will reserve a
subscription to Mills & Boon
Doctor Nurse Romances for you. Every
two months you will receive the latest
8 new titles, delivered direct to your door.
You don't pay extra for delivery. Postage and
packing is always completely Free.
There is no obligation or commitment –
you receive books only for
as long as you want to.

**It's easy! Fill in the coupon below and return it to
MILLS & BOON READER SERVICE, FREEPOST, P.O. BOX 236,
CROYDON, SURREY CR9 9EL.**

**Please note: READERS IN SOUTH AFRICA write to
Mills & Boon Ltd., Postbag X3010,
Randburg 2125, S. Africa.**

- -